D1433179

GALLOWS GHOST

A lone rider came out of the dark outlaw hideout in the Tenejos Hills. That rider called himself by the name of a man who'd been sentenced to die on the gallows twenty years before. Now he was seeking vengeance and his target was Marshal Colby Jackson—the son of the man who'd placed the rope around the rider's neck.

Peter B. Germano was born the oldest of six children in New Bedford, Massachusetts. During the Great Depression, he had to go to work before completing high school. It left him with a powerful drive to continue his formal education later in life, finally earning a Master's degree from Loyola University in Los Angeles in 1970. He sold his first Western story to A.A. Wyn's Ace Publishing magazine group when he was twenty years old. In the same issue of *Sure-Fire Western* (1/39) Germano had two stories, one by Peter Germano and the other by **Barry Cord**. He came to prefer the Barry Cord name for his Western fiction. When the Second World War came, he joined the U.S. Marine Corps. Following the war he would be called back to active duty, again as a combat correspondent, during the Korean conflict. In 1948 Germano began publishing a series of Western novels as Barry Cord, notable for their complex plots while the scenes themselves are simply set, with a minimum of description and quick character sketches employed to establish a wide assortment of very different personalities. The pacing, which often seems swift due to the adept use of a parallel plot structure (narrating a story from several different viewpoints), is combined in these novels with atmospheric descriptions of weather and terrain. *Dry Range* (1955), *The Sagebrush Kid* (1954), *The Iron Trail Killers* (1960), and *Trouble in Peaceful Valley* (1968) are among his best Westerns. "The great southwest . . ." Germano wrote in 1982, "this is the country, and these are the people that gripped my imagination . . . and this is what I have been writing about for forty years. And until I die I shall remain the little New England boy who fell in love with the 'West,' and as a man had the opportunity to see it and live in it."

GALLOWS GHOST

Barry Cord

GUNSMOKE

First published in the UK by Chivers

This hardback edition 2005
by BBC Audiobooks Ltd
by arrangement with
Golden West Literary Agency

ISBN 1 4056 8026 1

British Library Cataloguing in Publication Data available.

Printed and bound in Great Britain by
Antony Rowe Ltd., Chippenham, Wiltshire

I

Joe Wiley slammed the pole gate shut behind the bony rump of a four year old maverick and sleeved sweat from his young, reckless face. Rebellion made a hard streak in his gray eyes.

Turning, he shook a forefinger at his grinning partner sitting saddle a few feet away.

"Laugh!" he growled. "But I'm quittin', as of now! I'm fed up to here with fightin' horseflies, saddle sores an' chousin' muley-headed cows out of the brush! I'm tired of yore windy lies an' bad cookin'! I'm damn tired—" He paused to rake in a long breath. "I'm gonna take a dip in the crick, put on my best shirt an' take in the dance they're holdin' over to McNulty's place. Tim McNulty's christenin' his seventh boy an' he throws a real mean shindig!"

Slim Peters spat disdainfully over the ears of his patient bronc. "It's a twenty mile ride to McNulty's," he pointed out. "Besides, the boss'll likely be there—"

"Be hanged with that!" Joe said flatly. "I ain't seen another face 'cept yourn in three weeks. If Harvey Yellen don't like it when I show up, he knows what he can do with this job!"

Peters grunted. "No fool like a redheaded fool!" he observed philosophically. "Be back by noon tomorrer, or I'll have yore hide!" he added, raising his voice to reach the young puncher.

He swung his bronc away from the corral and put it for the water trough under the old oak. Peters was a lanky man of forty plus, bowed by too many years in the saddle and weathered by sun and blizzard until he looked like the hard and broken land about him. A Dragoon pistol was stuck in a cutaway holster at his right hip, but he was more prone to use the knife he wore in a sheath at his waist. He was an irascible sort, unpredictably moody, and for some strange reason he tolerated only redheaded Joe Wiley of all the Bar Y hands.

They made a pair, which accounted for their being here at the Bar Y's northernmost lineshack this hot July day, riding line and combing the Tenejos breaks for strays and outlaws.

About and around them loomed the Tenejos. They were savage, lonely hills broken and worn by weather, and they made a scythe sweep along this corner of Texas, shouldering eventually into the high plateau country of New Mexico.

Peters was midway to the water trough when he remembered he was out of the makings. He twisted in saddle. Joe was heading for the creek which ran below the linehouse—the redheaded puncher was pulling his shirt up over his head as he ran.

Peters raised his voice: "An' don't forget to buy some tobacco—"

GALLOWS GHOST

He saw Joe suddenly stop. The youngster had pulled his shirt free and he bunched it in his left hand now as he faced the thin stand of cottonwoods off to the left. His wiry torso gleamed whitely in the sunlight.

Something in Joe Wiley's tense stance touched a warning bell in Peters. He pulled his horse away from the trough and headed for the creek, and as he rode his hand rested on the butt of his gun.

The midafternoon sun laid its brutal heat across the corral where tawny dust raised by the restless, bawling steers sifted through the pole bars. A blue bottle fly came to rest on the back of Peters' gun hand, its feelers probing for salt. The leathery-faced puncher ignored it.

Joe was still facing the cottonwoods. He was a young, good-natured boy just two years shy of voting age. He packed a Colt on his hip and he was pretty good with it, shooting at tin cans.

Peters thought of this as he saw the rider emerge from the clump of cottonwoods. He rode at a walk toward Joe, his hands folded across the pommel of his saddle. From the distance separating them Peters noticed that the man seemed small and fragile sitting saddle of a big coal black stallion.

But Peters didn't relax. This was a hard land and a wild breed of men were known to tenant the Tenejos. Lying between New Mexico and Texas, crisscrossed only by forgotten trails and frequented only by men on the long dodge, the Tenejos had a bad reputation.

Slowly Peters eased his bronc to a stop behind Joe. The oncoming stranger was a thin man dressed in a black suit of broadcloth, white shirt, string tie. A flat-crowned black hat sat back from a high, shiny forehead. His face thin, sensitive, and his high cheekbones were the one spot of color in the otherwise sallow face.

7

He could have been a gambler strayed off the beaten trails. The long dark sideburn vising his jaws, the pencil moustache, the clothes, fitted the description. But the bone-handled Colts and the shell belts crossing under his coat were an off-key touch—they made Peters uneasy.

The stranger pulled up a few feet from Joe and ignoring the level regard of the young redhead he put his glance first on Peters, then in slow survey of the corral and lineshack.

His voice was low, modulated—the voice of an educated man. "This is a Bar Y linehouse, I presume?"

Joe Wiley's chuckle was spontaneous. "You presume right, mister. If the boss sent you up here to check on us, you kin tell him to—"

"Shut up!"

The stranger did not lift his voice, but there was an insolent dismissal of Joe in his curt interruption. He was looking at Peters now, judging the older man through eyes that were a bright, cold blue.

Joe started, taken back by the rider's attitude. Temper erased the good-natured grin from his face. "Now that's a hell of a way to—"

"*Shut up!*" The command was flat now, ugly.

Joe flung his shirt away, his mouth clamping tight. He started for the rider and behind him Peters' voice came a shade too late: "Joe! Look out for—"

The rider's foot slipped free from stirrup and arced up as Joe reached for him. The pointed boot toe caught Joe under the chin, crushing his larynx, snapping his head back. He stumbled, fighting to breathe, fumbling in shocked, blind rage for the Colt at his hip.

Peters was already dragging at his Dragoon. He didn't see the stranger draw; it was that fast. But he glimpsed a gout of black gunsmoke, flame-centered, a split second before

8

a massive blow his his chest. He was lifted from saddle and was dead before he hit the ground.

Joe was gagging, lifting his front sight over his holster top, when the muzzle blast from the rider above him spun him around. He didn't feel the impact of the second slug which smashed through the back of his head.

The big black minced away from the slowly thinning gunsmoke. The killer eyed the crumpled figures with dispassionate regard. Then he kneed the stallion on past them to the lineshack where he dismounted and went inside.

He found a coal oil lamp on a crude table and used the oil to soak the dry boards. He touched a match to the old newspaper he found on one of the two bunks and dropped it on the soaked floor.

From the corral he watched the smoke billow through the door. He coughed now, in a sudden sharp paroxysm which doubled him over the black's saddle horn. When it passed he raised pain-dulled eyes to the flames licking up around the door and slowly a brightness came back to his gaze.

He took a long slow breath. Then he reached down under his right leg for the Winchester in the saddle boot. He levered a shell into the chamber and killed Peters' horse which had drifted back to the water trough. He turned the muzzle to the corral. He fired methodically, like a man in a shooting gallery, aiming at clay targets. There were twenty-seven Bar Y steers penned in that enclosure—he killed them all.

Then he waited until the lineshack's roof caved in, sending a shower of sparks skyward. Satisfied, he turned the black toward the higher breaks of the Tenejos.

Sundown found him high among the broken hills. He broke out onto a narrow shelf jutting two thousand feet above the broad valley below and pulled up to let the big stallion blow.

9

Below him the evening shadows flowed like a dark tenuous stream toward the south—the river was a coil lost in the darkness of the country below.

A dry smile lifted the corners of his thin lips. "He'll come now, Rebel," he whispered softly to the black stallion. "When I get through with Harvey Yellen the Bar Y will be a bad memory—and Colby Jackson will be dead!"

The wind came cold from the ragged peaks behind him, taking his whisper with it, shredding it against the encroaching night.

II

THAT MARKED the beginning of the breakup of the Bar Y ranch.

On the twenty-first of July, Donna Yellen, only daughter of Harvey Yellen, saddled a dun mare she called Potluck and went riding. She rode alone, in a seeming hurry—and she didn't come back. She disappeared completely, as though she had ridden off the rim of the world.

Search for her was still in progress when Harvey's two sons, Marty and Larry, disappeared. A Bar Y line rider found Larry two days later, hanging from the branch of a live oak in a draw ten miles southwest of the main ranchhouse. His body was riddled with bullets.

Marty Yellen's body was never found.

The Bar Y hired twenty hands in the roundup season. All twenty hands were turned loose on the manhunt with added inducement of a five thousand dollar reward for the killer or killers behind the attack on the Bar Y. Five posses scoured the hills.

They found nothing. In their anger and frustration they burned whatever shack they ran across, hung two grim-lipped riders they stumbled upon watering spent horses at a small spring. But they found no trace of Donna, or her brother—and the attacks on the big spread were stopped only temporarily.

Two weeks later, while a few of his older hired hands were still riding the trackless Tenejos, Harvey Yellen was shot from ambush. He crawled all the way back to the ranchhouse, a matter of seven miles, dragging a bullet-smashed hip. He was out of his head for a week, and in bed for a month after—the doctor told him he would never get out of a chair again.

The big spread went to hell then. Faced with a killer no one saw—who moved with the patience and cunning of an Apache and killed with the same cruel and implacable anger—the old hands drifted away. The reward posters yellowed in the sun—the posses disintegrated—the sheriff, alone now, gave the Tenjos wide berth.

Clara Yellen finally wrote the letter. Tight-lipped, against her husband's wishes, she sat down one bitter night and wrote to the regional United States Marshal's office, addressing it to Marshal Colby Jackson.

A week later, on a cold and frosty November morning, a tall, broad-shouldered rider turned his horse into the Bar Y's ranchyard. He was a hard-looking man riding a hammer-headed roan horse. He was nearly thirty. Once he had been a reckless, thoughtless kid attending Colorado's College of Mines and Agriculture. He wasn't really interested in mining. His father supplied the money for his education and he sidetracked it into a good time.

Then his father died, and the money stopped coming. He sobered up in a hurry. He was big and tough, but he had brains, too, and he went to work in the government law office. Two years later his reputation haunted most of the men who rode the long dark trails. . . .

He dismounted in front of the wide veranda and glanced about him. Colby Jackson was no stranger to the Bar Y—the fabric of his life was woven here. He had known Harvey Yellen and his family for years—since his father's death the spread had become the nearest thing to home Jackson had.

Standing here now in front of the low rambling house he saw the air of neglect which hung like a pall over the one-time big ranch. Several men lounged around the bunkhouse. He recognized none of them. They eyed him with sullen suspicion, but no one came over to say hello.

The Bar Y was shot to hell, and looked it. Charred remains of the big barn lay scattered beyond the almost empty corrals; the tool and harness sheds were gone. Harvey's gig lay rusting in the back yard.

A cold wind scurried dried oak leaves across the frozen earth. From somewhere behind the house a dog lifted his voice in lonesome howl.

Colby felt a shiver go down his back. He went up the steps and Clara Yellen, small and straight and gray-haired, met him at the door. She looked tired and despair had etched deep lines around her mouth.

But her eyes lighted up as she greeted him.

"Colby—Colby—" She held out a small hand to him and clung to him; he felt her shiver and his heart went out to her. Clara Yellen was only five feet two, but she had always stood tall—she was a strong woman in a land that needed strength. But he felt her need now, the note of despair in her voice.

"He's in the bedroom," she said. She took Colby's hat and summoned a welcoming smile to her lips. "I'm glad you came, Colby."

"Nothing could have kept me away," Colby said. "You know that."

He followed her to the bedroom where Harvey Yellen, looking oddly shrunken and old, hitched himself up against the solid oak headboard.

"Colby! Damn you, I didn't want you to see me—like this!"

The Marshal's eyes were dark with understanding. There had always been a strong pride in Harvey Yellen—a pride in himself and a pride in doing. He had carved the Bar Y out of this wilderness with brawn as well as brains and carried on with a stubborn persistence that had survived drought and blizzard and hard times. . . .

Colby pulled a chair up by the bed and listened to Harvey's story. Listened quietly while the cattleman poured out a tale of cruel, systematic destruction.

"How many ride with him, Colby, I don't know. Not many have seen him—those who have are dead. But he comes and goes—"

"Who?"

Harvey looked surprised. "Oh . . . I thought Clara wrote—" He glanced at his wife, standing in the background—then he sighed. "He calls himself Doc Wesley—he's holed up somewhere in the Tenejos."

Colby frowned. The name had an odd ring of familiarity, and he sensed that Harvey expected him to know the man. But his identity escaped him.

"The Bar Y's through—finished!" Harvey was muttering. "But my daughter—she's still alive. He's got her with him, in the Tenejos!"

A deep and shame-filled hurt tortured him. "I don't care

what's happened to her, Colby. Find her! Bring her back home!"

Colby nodded. He was thinking of the young woman he had known, barely out of her teens.

"Why?" he asked, quietly, puzzled. "Who is this Doc Wesley? What's he got against you?"

Harvey Yellen looked at his wife. He drew a thin, rasping breath, shook his head. "Not me, Colby—*you!*"

Colby straightened in his chair.

"It sounds crazy, I know," Harvey muttered. "Only a crazy man—or a dead man—would think this way. But— it's you he's after, Colby!"

The Deputy Marshall's eyes held a bleak questioning. "Why me? I've never even met the man—"

"Listen," the crippled cattleman cut in. "A long time ago, while you were at that engineering college in Colorado, your father and I worked on the same job. We were both mining engineers for the I.O.U. mine in the now forgotten gold camp called Apache Creek." He smiled weakly. "You don't remember that camp in the Tenejos, eh? Few do. The gold strike petered just before the War. It's a ghost town now. Not many even know where it is."

Colby leaned forward. "What has all this to do with Doc Wesley?"

Harvey turned. He fumbled under his pillow for a letter which he handed to the Marshal.

Wondering, Colby Jackson read the grim message written in a fine Spencerian hand:

"*My Dear Harvey Yellen:*

If you want to know what's become of your other son, and if you wish to see your daughter again, send for Tom Jackson's boy. The United States Marshal whose reputation throws such a long shadow across Texas. When he comes, tell him to ride alone to Apache Creek. You will remember, of course, what happened there on the 10th of November, 1860. There's a slab in boothill I want Jackson's boy to see—and remember. Send for him, Harvey—if you wish to see your daughter again."

It was signed *Doc Wesley*.

Jackson reached out and slowly handed Harvey the letter. There was a harsh note to his question: "This Doc Wesley—who is he? Just what happened at Apache Creek?"

Harvey licked his lips. An odd fear made a streak across his lined face. "A man named Doc Wesley was hanged there. Lynched by an angry mob of miners. The I.O.U. was one of the few mines still paying off when this Doc Wesley placed a charge of dynamite in the entrance and blew it up. Your father saw him do it. Fifteen men were trapped and killed in that explosion. Your father and I tried to stop the lynching—"

"Then Doc Wesley is dead?" Jackson interrupted. His eyes were hard. "You say you saw him hang?"

Harvey nodded. "I saw him die. He was guilty—no doubt about it. Although we never found out why he did it. He swore with the rope around his neck that he had his good reasons for wanting to close the I.O.U. And after your father testified to what he had seen, he swore to get Tom. He died with that on his lips."

Colby closed his eyes for a moment. Outside, the cold wind pried at loose shutters.

"I want my girl back, Colby," Clara Yellen whispered from across the room. There were tears in her eyes. "No matter what's happened, I want her back—"

Colby closed his eyes. He nodded slowly and got to his feet.

"I'll find her," he promised.

He rode away from the Bar Y under an overcast sky. The wind was spitting the first snow of the year when he headed for the Tenejos looming dark against the cold gray sky.

III

SNOW CAME early that year to the Tenejos. It began with a dry powdery fall riding a howling wind. It sifted along the hard and broken land, piling up into little ridges, leaving stretches of gray and naked rock that were like the bare bones of this hard country.

Colby Jackson rode down the lost empty street of Apache Creek with the day fading fast behind him. He rode with the ghost of his father whom he remembered only as a voice, deep and chuckling and gentle . . . A man who even in his disappointment had tried to understand Colby.

He had died while Colby was still in school, and now Colby understood how little he had known his father. Some of his hopes were buried here. . . . A part of his life had been lived here.

Yet, looking about him, it was hard for Colby to believe that this gold camp had once been a flourishing community of five thousand people. The tents were long gone, struck and packed away—the jerry-built wooden structures had long since bowed to the elements. A few walls and their foundations straggled along the gulch, close by the frozen coils of Apache Creek—the long ago laughter and the tears were ghosts of echoes on the biting wind.

The canyon walls were pockmarked with old shafts, as though a company of gnomes had lived here. Here and there abandoned narrow gauge tracks led out of some of the bigger mine shafts, ending at the steep pitch into the canyon. The remains of a stamp mill, huge iron stacks lying rusted and uncaring, stood like the bones of some stricken giant down by the creek.

The snow drifted down in a fine whisper and the ghosts of the men who had lived and died here seemed to mutter in the wind. A cold prickle touched Marshal Jackson's spine as he reflected that his father had once walked this narrow and forgotten street in a time now lost forever.

He rode slowly along the upslanting road, his senses momentarily dulled by crowding memories and regrets. His sheepskin coat was unbuttoned and his ungloved right hand lay on his pommel. He knew he was dealing with a man who obeyed no rules, and he had taken precautions—but for the moment he was riding the backtrails of memory.

Up past the sagging walls of the mercantile store he paused and sat waiting. He had the prickly feeling of being watched, and yet he saw nothing move in that silent, still ghost town that was slowly whitening under the fading light of day.

His breath made its little white banner on the cold air. His horse tossed his head impatiently, his long muscles shivering.

The Marshal rode on past the ruins of the "GOLDEN GOOSE SALOON" and by "MARIE'S HAT SHOPPE."

Past the broken-down walls of the sheriff's office, the sign still readable after these many years.

The bones of this dead town lay naked to his questing gaze. The ghosts of long ago hopes and bitter frustrations swirled in the thickening spit of snow. Colby's thoughts went to Harvey Yellen, lying broken and bitter on his bed, and of a girl he had known almost as a sister. She was probably dead, he thought bleakly, buried somewhere in these cold hills.

A dead man's name had been signed to that letter. But it was no dead man who had shot Harvey. And it would be no ghost he would meet here!

He saw no one in his long slow ride up that canyon street toward the high ground at the head of it. Now the straggle of what had been the main business section of Apache Creek lay behind and below him. The old I.O.U. mine with its sagging trestle was above him, on his right. To his left, across a narrow gully, on a small ridge of earth, the remarkably preserved one room schoolhouse still stood.

Apache Creek's boothill was situated almost under the sagging mine trestle which once had crossed over to the other side of the creek. Colby rode down between the pillars of stone marking the entrance to the cemetery and paused, letting his eyes pick out names on the slate slabs.

The character of the one-time brawling gold camp could be read in this graveyard, in the blunt epitaphs chiseled into the headstones. The one he was looking for stood by itself, off in a corner. Leaning forward, Jackson read the old inscription:

DOC WESLEY
HANGED DECEMBER 10, 1851
AN EDUCATED MAN GONE TO HELL.

The grave was here, and by rights the moldering bones of Doc Wesley should be here, too . . . and yet Doc Wesley, it seemed, was not dead. He rode the bleak hills of the Tenejos, and he rode in revenge.

Jackson waited, knowing that somewhere in this forgotten town a mad man was watching him. He waited, listening to the wind and the snow, and after an interval he reached under his coat for the makings and his cold fingers spun a cigaret. He was bringing the cupped match flame to it when the girl called; harshly and without hope:

"Colby . . . Colby Jackson!"

He turned to face the voice and his hand held a Colt. It was an instinctive motion. . . .

He glimpsed Donna Yellen on the trestle above him. It had been five years since he had last seen her, and she had been a leggy, pigtailed girl of sixteen then. She was a woman now, standing tall and stiff on the trestle, and just behind her a small man loomed, black suit and string tie and thin, ascetic face. . . .

The bullet hit Jackson high, knocking him out of his roan's saddle. He fell on his side, numbed to the impact, and tried to roll away and bring his Colt up to line on that blurred, arrogant face. He heard the girl's voice, from seemingly far away, and puzzling. . . . "No . . . no more . . . you promised me, Doc!" And then the second bullet slammed into him and he collapsed and lay still.

The man on the trestle laughed. "An eye for an eye, Jackson!" he muttered. "Claw for claw!" He pulled the girl toward him, onto the path above the road. She went like a sleepwalker, face white as the falling snow.

The horses waited in the darkness of the old I.O.U. mine shaft. The girl mounted Potluck and Doc Wesley stepped up into the saddle of the big black stallion. They rode away along the dim and narrow trail looping high

19

along the gulch wall, turning finally to snake over the ridge. They rode without looking back.

The snowfall thickened and fell softly now, sticking and whitening the canyon floor. The roan trotted back to the fallen figure. His whinny was uneasy. He nosed the big man lying still and huddled on that hard earth. He whickered yearningly. There was no answer from Jackson. Only the soft chittering of the falling snow as it began to ridge along the United States Marshal's body. . . .

Maury Bittering unpacked the beef quarter from his pack animal and hung it from the rafters of his shed. He saw to the horses first and then turned to the cabin in the small grassy valley in the Tenejos.

He had pushed the animals the last hours, bucking the snow that began to drift in the low places. Now he was home. He saw the welcome curl of smoke from the stone chimney he had built himself, and his stride quickened.

It had been a long ride down to the valley of the Pecos. He had shot the first beef he had come across, a Bar Y steer, and taken what he needed of the animal, leaving the rest for the scavengers. He had made his sortie after meat boldly, with no fear of reprisal from the big ranch.

It had taken almost a day's riding to get back here. He was a slat-thin, gaunt man with lined, weathered features— a man past forty, past arrogance, past hope. He was a fugitive who had found anchor in the anonymity of the Tenejos. . . .

He opened the cabin door and the warmth from the stove felt good after the long cold ride. He walked past the glowing range where a dutch oven oozed an aroma of rabbit stew. He poured himself a cup of coffee and warmed his hands around the tin cup. After a while he went out again.

He knew where he would find his wife.

He followed the steep narrow path behind the woodshed, up a small oak-covered knoll. He found her kneeling beside the wooden cross he had erected, a year ago, over the grave of his only child.

He paused and stood over her, seeing the thin body under the shawl and homespun, noting the dull grayshot brown hair, the creased cheek. Lucy Bittering was only thirty-three. She looked twenty years older.

A hard anger shook Maury at the injustice of it, of the punishment a man brought on those he loved. After a while he fought his anger down and knelt beside her. He put a gentle hand on her shoulder. She didn't stir.

"It's snowing," he said.

"Susan liked snow," she whispered. There was a fathomless quality to her voice, a far-away inflection.

"She's beyond caring whether it snows or not," he said, and there was an unnecessary roughness to his tone, an armor he drew over his own deep and unhealing hurt. "But she's better off than we are, Lucy. Come."

He lifted her to her feet and she did not protest. They walked back to the cabin. The snow swirled across the small valley and felt cold against his face. Lucy walked like an old woman, with no spring to her step.

They were coming around the woodshed when Maury saw the rider. He loomed like a ghost from among the cedars, drifting toward them. Maury pushed Lucy behind him and his hand reached under his coat, gripping the cold handle of his .45. He drew it and thumbed the hammer back, fear slitting his eyes, choking the breath in him.

"*So they've finally found me?*" he thought, and there was a bleak despair in him.

The horse drifted closer, lifting its head and nickering eagerly now. And Maury, peering through the veil of snow, saw a big man slumped forward on that roan's neck —a man he didn't know.

He moved cautiously, still holding his cocked Colt ready. Snow plastered the man's coat, but there was a reddish tinge to it. . . . He felt the roan nudge him, almost as though the animal were urging him to do something about the man on his back.

Maury growled, "Hold it. I'll take a look at him. . . ."

He pouched his Colt and reached up to pull the wounded man from saddle. The rider seemed rooted there, his fingers stiffened in the roan's mane. Maury had to twist them loose. Slowly he eased Colby Jackson out of saddle, staggering a little under the Marshal's weight.

"Lucy." He turned to the woman behind him. "Help me get him into the house. This man's hurt."

Together they dragged Jackson into the cabin, laid him out on the straw ticking. They worked the coat off Colby. Maury shook his head at what he saw.

"Oughta be dead," he marveled. "Don't see how he lasted this long, Lucy. But, maybe . . . he looks tougher'n an oak tree. Some gunslinger on the run from the law, probably. . . ." There was an aching sympathy in his tone. "Let's see what we can do for him."

His wife put water on the stove to heat. While she busied herself Maury worked Colby's boots off. The big man stirred then, a pair of blue-gray eyes opened and measured Maury with long regard. They seemed to be probing, trying to remember. Then a small smile edged Jackson's hard lips—he made a thank-you gesture with his hand. And passed out again.

Maury pulled Jackson's other boot off, then stood up to drape Jackson's bullet-torn coat across the back of a chair.

Jackson's wallet dropped out and a bright object winked up at Maury from the inner flap.

Maury looked at the silver United States Marshal's badge, his face stiffening, fear draining the blood from it. Then he drew his Colt and thumbed the hammer back, bringing the muzzle down on the unconscious man on on the bunk.

His wife came to him, grabbing his arm, pulling it down. "Maury!" Her voice was shocked. "Why?"

"Lawman!" he said harshly.

She looked down at Jackson, her eyes dark with concern. "He's badly hurt. He may even die."

"I'm not going back to hang!" he said stonily.

She held onto his gun arm. "He may not be after you. And—you can't kill again! A helpless man! I can't stand it, Maury! Not again!"

He felt her tremble and after a while he drew a deep, shuddering breath. He had broken out of Stony Point jail, killing a guard in his escape. He had served more than six years of a ten years sentence for armed stage robbery.

Six hopeless years behind gray prison walls, behind cold bars. For one mistake. He had needed money for Lucy right after Susan had been born—he had let himself get talked into going along with two men he had met in a saloon in Caldwell. They left him holding the bag, and he had talked at the trial—he got ten years. The two men had a price put on their heads, but they were never picked up.

He had served six out of the ten years sentence, then he had broken out. He had found Lucy and young Susan and fled from the law, heading for California. Susan had died of fever on the way. They were close to the Tenejos when it happened; they drove on, no longer caring, until they found this little valley, hidden away, which offered a hopeless sort of sanctuary. Maury had decided then he would run no longer.

He looked down at Jackson now and slowly slid his Colt back into holster. Lucy Bittering gave him a tremulous smile. She left him and went to the stove for the hot water.

"Help me?" she asked softly, and Maury obeyed, like a wooden man, stiff-jointed and unfeeling.

IV

THE CANDLE GLOWED in the cracked windowpane. Colby Jackson stood under the cedars, leaning on the axe handle. He could see the warm, flickering glow against the glass and he thought of the woman in that shack whose face had lightened during the weeks he had been here.

Snow lay like a white veil over the land. His breath was frosty. Slowly the weakness was working out of his muscles. He no longer felt exhausted after a few minutes chopping firewood—he could feel the strength coming back into his arms and shoulders and legs, although at times the puckered scars in his side and chest pained him.

He gathered up the firewood and started for the cabin. It was time he left them, he thought: He was able to ride, and his roan was getting restless in the lean-to behind the cabin.

And the memory of Donna Yellen standing beside the black-garbed killer on the I.O.U. trestle haunted him. He had to find her. He had promised Harvey Yellen and his wife.

He had tried to get information from Maury, but the

man was uncommunicative on some things. Doc Wesley? Maury had shrugged. Sure, he had heard the name. Everyone in the Tenejos had heard of Doc. And everyone stayed shy of him. A lone wolf. Yeah—it was rumored he had a girl living with him— A strange young girl—

Colby tried to pin Bittering down. "Where does he hang out, Maury?"

"The Tenejos are big," the small man had said. He had looked Colby squarely in the eye. "You want Doc Wesley that much?"

"That much," Colby nodded, and his voice was bleak and savage.

"Two places I heard of," Maury had muttered reluctantly. "The Morgan place . . . or Portigee Joe's, in Big Pine . . . ."

Colby had never heard of either place, but he had dropped the conversation, sensing Maury's growing reluctance.

He was halfway to the cabin when he spotted the two riders emerging from the pine-shrouded trail into the clearing. They pulled up sharply as they saw him.

Jackson stood still, the firewood in the curl of his left arm. His right hand held the double-bitted axe. He watched them split and ride toward him at a walk, and it occurred to him that every man in the Tenejos rode warily; they were either the hunted, or the hunters.

The man on Colby's left, mounted on a jugheaded buckskin horse, was older and shorter than his companion. He seemed shapeless in an old sheepskin coat and crushed Stetson. A brown wool muffler was knotted under his grizzled chin, protecting his ears from the cold.

He slipped his right hand free of his coat pocket as he came up and Colby noticed that it was bare—and knew, too, that the butt of a Colt lay within easy reach of that horny hand.

He eyed Colby with narrowing distrust while his companion, a taller, raw-boned man with a ragged, drooping moustache giving him years he did not own, worked a chaw of tobacco back into his right cheek.

He sniffed as though he had a bad cold. "Who are you, mister?"

"No one you know," Colby answered shortly. He had a grim suspicion these men were looking for Maury, and he hoped Lucy would not come to the door. . . .

Beaver turned to the shorter man. "Right sassy, ain't he?" he drawled. "Reckon we oughta cut him down to size, Odds?"

Odds Hawley shook his head. His eyes were bright on Colby's face. "You look like somebody I oughta remember," he muttered. Then: "We're looking for Maury. We was told this was his place."

Colby kept his expression blank. Maury had ridden out early in the morning for a place called Ten-Spot Smith's to pick up supplies. Smith's place was, he inferred, a hole-in-the-wall in the back draws of the Tenejos, frequented by owlhooters on their way to or from sanctuary in Mexico.

"I'm not Maury," he said slowly.

"Reckon you ain't!" Beaver snapped. He was an impatient sort of man. "We know Maury." He started to dismount and Colby said softly, "I wouldn't do that, fella. There isn't anyone named Maury around here."

Beaver gave Jackson a long slow look. He saw the way Jackson held the axe and he got the cold feeling that he wouldn't quite get to his holstered gun if he tried to push this further. The big man's eyes, measuring him with cold and watchful regard, held Beaver motionless. He glanced at Hawley, waiting for his companion's cue.

Odds Hawley sighed. "We'll be back, fella—"

They neck-reined their mounts around and rode away. The tautness in Colby Jackson's muscles faded—he felt a sag of spirits. If they ran into Maury at Ten Spot Smith's —or on the trail—?

He heard the door open and turning he saw Lucy framed in it. Her eyes were troubled.

"Those men, Colby! I heard one of them call the other Odds?"

"That name mean anything to you?"

She nodded. "The men who were with my husband when they held up the stage were named Beaver and Odds Hawley. Maury told me about them—" She saw the lack of understanding in Jackson's face and she said tiredly, "Come inside. I'll tell you why Maury and I are here, hiding in this wilderness. . . ."

She told Colby the story of Maury's imprisonment and his escape. And of her husband's hatred of the law—and of their daughter, Susan, whose body lay in the grave on the hill.

Colby listened with compassion. Maury Bittering, it seemed, had paid deeply for his one misstep.

His voice was gentle as Lucy finished. "I owe you both my life. Nothing I can do to help you will ever repay that."

"I'm worried about Maury," she said. "Those men are looking for him. If they run into him at the store—"

"I'll ride out after him," Colby said. "Just in case."

She turned away, a shadow in her eyes. "I—I was to give you these in the morning. Maury said it was all right."

Colby waited, frowning slightly. He watched her go to an old wood chest in the corner and open it. He saw her take out his gun belt—and his Colt. And when she came to him she had his badge in her hand.

He took them, not saying anything.

She smiled sadly. "We knew you were a law officer the day you got here. Maury thought you were after him."

"And yet you helped me?"

"I've had enough of killing," she whispered. "And Maury would never find peace again, that way. Perhaps we never shall—again. There's a reward on his head. I've seen the posters. You see, Colby—he killed a guard when he broke out of prison."

Jackson nodded slowly, remembering now. . . . He had seen Maury's description on one of the posters in a sheriff's office in the Panhandle. But he knew he couldn't bring himself to take the man in.

He took his badge from her and looked at it and his face was cold and wooden—then he gave it back to her. "Hold it for me," he said tonelessly, and she understood. For the time he was without his badge he could be just Colby Jackson, in debt to Maury Bittering.

He strapped on his gun belt, checked his Colt. Then he placed a gentle hand on Lucy Bittering's shoulder.

"We'll be back in time for supper," he reassured her. "Don't you go worrying."

She walked to the door with him and waited there until he rode by, mounted on his rested roan stallion. She felt strangely at peace, as though this big man, somehow, had instilled in her a deep and lasting confident. He was strong and yet gentle, and she believed him when he told her not to worry. . . . Then she thought of Susan and what the girl might have become, if she had lived, and a pang went through her.

She had not gone up to the grave since the day Jackson had come to them. Had not felt the hopeless need driving her to inconsolable mourning at Susan's burial place. The big man had brought purpose into her empty life—those first days in which he had hovered between life and death had been a challenge.

Now, as she watched him ride toward the pines at the far end of the clearing, she felt the need, once more, to visit Susan's grave.

She went back inside for her shawl. The wind had taken on a bitter edge and the misty sun had gone. . . . Clouds were piling up over the northern rises. She walked briskly up the path to the small knoll, her gray shapeless skirt flapping against her legs. She felt lighter and younger and her eyes had a sort of sparkle to them again.

She knelt by that small headboard and closed her eyes and prayed . . . and then she just stayed there, thinking nothing, not feeling the bitter edge of the wind . . . feeling only a release and a peace she had not known in years.

The man's voice shook her out of her reverie. It was harsh and disrespectful, striking on her ears.

"You'll get housemaid's knees, staying down like that, ma'am!" A hand closed roughly over her shoulder and she was dragged to her feet.

She tried to twist free, a startled cry escaping her. Beaver's long, ugly face sneered at her. Odds Hawley stood by, watching.

"We waited until he rode off, then came back," Beaver said. "He's gone to fetch Maury, ain't he?"

She shook her head, terror growing inside her. "No, no—I don't know where he's going—"

"He's gone for Maury!" Hawley cut in coldly. "We could have followed him. But this way it'll be more private." He looked at his partner and laughed. "That's what we want, ain't it, Odds? Privacy."

Odds grinned wolfishly. "Yeah." Then he shivered and looked up at the sky. "No need to wait up here. Let's get her down to the cabin. . . ."

V

TEN SPOT SMITH's place was a hole-in-the wall log cabin tucked back in a narrow canyon. There was a rough wagon road leading to it, used by unscrupulous freighters willing to risk their necks for a quick buck and high profits.

The necessities came high at Ten Spot's, but most of the men who stopped by for supplies could pay the price. Those who couldn't kept riding.

Winter snows had closed most of the trails through the Tenejos and made the wagon road impassable. Only those who made the Tenejos their home moved at all, and some of them came to Ten Spot's for whiskey and a game of cards to break the monotony of the long winter days.

Maury was alone at the far end of the plank bar, brooding over a glass of cheap rotgut whiskey. Smith was reading a month old newspaper. . . . In the back his Indian wife singsonged an ancient tune as she sat in front of the blanket she was weaving. Samples of her handiwork hung on the walls. . . .

At a corner table behind the pot-bellied stove four men played cards. They had just come inside and they made a noisy change to the usual cabin solitude.

Maury finished his drink and glanced toward the window. It had turned gray outside and he had the premonition of more snow in the offing.

Ten Spot Smith came over and started to refill his glass. "On the house," he said. He kept his voice low; he didn't want the men at the table to hear.

Maury shook his head. "Thanks," he said quietly. "But I should be getting back." The liquor he had consumed gave him no glow; he felt somewhat depressed and dull.

Smith reached under the counter and placed a small batch of folded newspapers in front of Maury. "Somethin' for you an' the missus to read." He smiled. "Ain't much to do for Christmas celebration here, but if you an' Mrs. Bittering care to stop by for eggnog . . . ?"

He saw the tortured look that came over Maury's face and he let the matter drop. A loud voice in the group at the table yelled for another bottle and he brought it to them.

Maury looked at the old newspapers. Christmas! A time for gaiety—a holiday for children. A bitter hopelessness flooded him, leaving a taste like bile in his mouth.

He picked up the newspapers, made a roll of them and thrust them into his coat pocket. A gunny sack holding the supplies he had ordered when he had entered lay at his feet. He bent to pick it up and go.

Smith came back to the bar. He seemed vaguely worried. "You haven't finished your drink," he said loudly. He pushed the glass toward Maury and indicated the men at the table with his eyes. "Trouble brewing," he muttered.

Maury eased the gunny sack down. He had paid little attention to the four men at the far end of the room. All but one were hidden by the stove in the middle of the floor.

The backlash of their talk caught up with him now and he listened for a moment, his lips curling. "Bunch of goddam fools!" he muttered. "Always got to get bigger than the rest!"

Smith kept his troubled voice low. "Only thing that'll come out of that kind of talk is trouble. Big trouble, Maury. It'll bring the Rangers into the Tenejos, see if it don't!"

Maury stifled a bitter laughter. Hell, the law was in the Tenejos now! At least one representative was. A man he had been forced to take care of. He thought of the big man back at the shack with Lucy . . . a man he knew only as Colby. A tight-mouthed hombre who moved like some big cat yet was strangely gentle, always courteous.

The U.S. Marshal must have missed his gun and his badge, but not once had he asked about them.

Who was he after? Why had he come to the Tenejos? Doc Wesley, it seemed. Maury's inner thoughts must have been reflected in his face for Smith said: "Something botherin' you, Maury? Those two hombres who were in here early this mornin', askin' about you? I thought they were friends of yores, or I wouldn't have—"

"Who?" Maury's attention narrowed on the implication of Smith's information. "Someone askin' for me?"

Smith nodded. "Didn't give names, when I asked them. Just said they knew you. Best I can describe them was that the older one was short, the other chewed tobacco an' was taller." He added slowly. "Looked about as mean as any who stop in here—"

Maury felt a rising panic. Smith's description could fit almost anyone. But for two years now Maury had been expecting Beaver and Odds Hawley—sooner or later men of that ilk made their sojourn into the Tenejos.

He finished his drink and picked up his sack of supplies and said almost curtly: "Thanks, Smith . . ."

"Just a minnit, hombre!" The man who had detached

himself from the group at the card table was a heavy-shouldered, muscular man a head taller than Maury. He had a square, time-gullied face from which pale yellow eyes surveyed the world with sneering arrogance.

He came walking toward the bar, wiping his roan moustache with the back of a hair-tufted hand. His sheepskin coat was unbuttoned and the butt of a Remington .45 lay snug in a cutaway black leather holsters.

"We're takin' a poll, Maury," he said. He had the kind of voice that instinctively made strangers tense—the sneering challenge was a part of him.

Maury picked up the gunny sack and hitched it over his shoulder. He knew this man from previous mettings in Smith's—knew him as "Hash" McCoy, one of the Morgan brothers' bunch of horse thieves. A quarrelsome gent whose claim to a fast gun hand was borne out by his still being alive in a land where men lived by the gun.

Maury waited, holding back the small panic which Smith's words had raised in him. He had to get back before Beaver and Odds Hawley showed up. The Marshal might help. But he had no gun. Maury had given Lucy strict orders to keep his gun locked up in the old trunk.

Hash's yellowed teeth showed in a non-humorous grin. "We're organizin', Maury. Gettin' all the gunhands in the Tenejos together—"

"Not me," Maury cut in brusquely. "I was never much of a joiner." He started to turn away, but McCoy put a heavy hand on his shoulder.

"It ain't a question of choice," he said. His voice had softened and taken on a dangerous edge. "You heard of Doc Wesley?"

Maury said: "Yeah." He was a small man with a low boiling point; it had gotten him into trouble many times.

"He's got an idea," McCoy snapped. "It makes sense

to me. Makes sense to everybody I talked to. Organize the
Tenejos, Doc said. There's enough of us hiding out in these
goddam hills to run this whole Pecos country, if we band
together. Alone we're nothin'—"

Maury shrugged Hash's hand off his shoulder. "I ain't
a joiner," he repeated curtly. "I don't want to run anything."

MCoy snickered. "Lissen to him, boys! Maury doesn't
want to run anything." He turned back to the small man.
"You won't ben runnin' anythin', Maury. There'll be others
who'll do that. You just takes orders. Or—"

"Or?" Maury's voice held the edge of a bitter temper.

"Or you leave the Tenejos!" McCoy snarled.

Maury licked his lips. It had taken him almost fifty
years to learn to control his temper; now it didn't matter.

"I've had my day, Hash," he muttered between his teeth.
"I've hung up my gun rig. I wouldn't be of any use to Doc—"

"Doc'll be the judge of that!" McCoy snapped. He hooked
a finger between the top buttons of Maury's coat, jerked
the little man to him. "There ain't gonna be place for
fence-straddlers in the Tenejos. You got one choice. You ride
with us!"

A horse whickered softly at the rack outside and McCoy
lifted his gaze to the ice-rimmed window. Maury took
this break in McCoy's attention to jerk free. He started to
back away from the bar, fighting the anger in him. . . . He
didn't want trouble with McCoy now. Not while Beaver and
Hawley were looking for him—

"I'll do my own choosing, Hash!" he snarled, and turned
to leave. Then he stopped as though he had run up against
an invisible wall and relief mingled with a sharp surprise
as he recognized the big man coming through the doorway.

Jackson paused just inside the small room. His gun rode

in the tied-down holster on his thigh—Maury almost expected to see the glint of his badge on his coat.

Something must have happened back at the cabin, he thought and he tried to read the Marshal's face.

McCoy took a long step away from the bar, his face twisted in questioning scowl. Talk at the table beyond the stove ceased abruptly. Maury wondered if any of these owlhooters had recognized this newcomer as a United States Marshal. If they did, he reflected grimly, their lives wouldn't be worth the price of a wickless candle.

Jackson immediately sensed the studied watchfulness in that close, smoke-hazed room. He moved toward Maury without hurry, a big man used to violence and the threat of it—and not of a temperament to eagerly avoid it.

He reached out his left hand and took the gunny sack from Maury's shoulder. His voice was gentle. "Lucy's waiting for you—"

McCoy stepped between them. "Jest a minnit, fella. Who in hell are you? I haven't seen you around before?"

"Haven't seen you either," Jackson replied. There was a curtness in his tone that acted like a slap in the face to McCoy. Few men had ever talked to him like that and then turned their back on him, as this big stranger was doing.

He shoved his hand under his coat for his Remington and it lay cocked in his hand as he stepped back, bracing himself along the bar.

"You see me now, fella!" he said harshly. "An' you'll do some powwowin'. The Tenejos are exclusive. I want to hear yore pedigree—from the beginnin'!"

Jackson had paused. He turned slowly to eye this heavy-shouldered, craggy-faced outlaw against the bar. He didn't want trouble with McCoy, and he would have cooked up a phony background if Maury had given him time. But the little man moved before Jackson could reply.

Maury spun around. His left elbow jabbed into Mc-Coy's stomach and at the same time his right hand swept upward, deflecting the bigger man's gun. There was a heavy report in the room as McCoy fired a shot into the ceiling. Then Jackson was crowding him. His gun made a blurred arc, ending abruptly behind McCoy's left ear.

Hash McCoy folded along the bar front. Jackson wheeled and pushed Maury ahead of him, toward the door. His leveled Colt put its cold challenge to the men caught by surprise around the card table. He voiced no threat, but no man moved.

Maury went out and the big Marshal followed. They mounted and wheeled away from the rack, losing themselves almost immediately behind the screen of timber through which the road led.

VI

MAURY'S FACE was troubled as he glanced at the stony-faced Marshal. The powerful roan stallion Jackson rode was moving fast along the icy trail and Maury's horse was having trouble keeping up.

"Whoa!" he called out sharply, digging in his heels against the dun's flanks and cutting in alongside the lawman. "Hold it, Colby. Ease that big cayuse of yores down to a walk. What's the hurry?"

Jackson looked over this shoulder. "Couple of hombres stopped by the cabin, asking for you. Name of Beaver and Odds Hawley—"

Maury stiffened. Fear made his eyes bright and panicky. "Lucy . . . ?"

Jackson eased back and put a reassuring hand on Maury's shoulder. "She's all right, Maury. But I've got a hunch they'll be back. Perhaps I should have stayed at the cabin with her and waited for you. But your wife was worried about you. And she told me a lot of things."

Maury said bitterly: "About my past?"

Jackson shrugged. "I want you to know that I didn't come to the Tenejos looking for you."

Maury's eyes held a stony glaze. "Doc Wesley?"

Jackson nodded. "A man I never met, or knew—a killer whose body should be in a grave in Apache Creek. You know him?"

"I saw him once," Maury muttered. "In Smith's place. He doesn't look like much. A small man, like me—and about my age. Coughed a lot. I'd say he had lung fever. Wears two guns, dresses in black, like some preacher." Maury's grin held little humor. "From what I hear he does his preaching behind those Colts—"

"Hear anything else?" Jackson cut in impatiently. "Who the men are behind the raids on the Bar Y? Hear anything about a girl and a boy, around twenty, riding with Doc?"

Maury shook his head. "I hear rumors about a girl riding with Doc. I never saw her. About the boy—?" He shrugged. "Smith might know—he knows most of what goes on in the Tenejos. The Morgan brothers, Corby and Moose, are behind the raids on the Bar Y. Doc Wesley started it, I hear—something about wanting to get back at Harvey Yellen for something. I—I never bothered too much with those stories, Colby. But I know the Morgan bunch has been having easy pickings of Bar Y beef since last summer. . . ."

Jackson nodded grimly. "Stands to reason," he muttered.

37

"One man couldn't have smashed Bar Y as badly as it has been smashed. Not even a madman, or a ghost." He smiled bleakly at Maury's look. "Doc Wesley is of the Tenejos, Maury. Where does he hole up in bad weather?"

Maury shrugged. "I told you once—in Portigee Joe's place. But I don't know where that is, exactly. Somewhere north of Big Baldy." He frowned. "The Morgans would know, though."

"Why would they know?"

Maury cast a glance over his shoulder. "That was Hash McCoy you slugged in Ten Spot Smith's place. A bad hombre with a big mouth. But he rides for the Morgans, sort of segundo for them. The Morgans have been in the Tenejos for years, long before I got here. They've got a so-called horse spread in Black Cat Canyon, this side of Big Baldy mountain. Up to this summer they kept their thieving strictly to horseflesh. . . . I hear they got more than a thousand head of Bar Y beef stashed in several of the small canyons close to their spread, waiting for the mountain passes to clear. They been selling them in Mexico."

"Corby and Moose Morgan," Jackson muttered. "I'll remember them."

"Remember Hash McCoy, too," Maury warned. "He's a bad hombre to tangle with; he'll never forget what you did to him." He reached out and put a hand on Jackson's shoulder. "There's something else brewing in the Tenejos. When you came in Hash was trying to force me to join up—"

"Join up?"

"Something about the Tenejos organizing under Doc Wesley," Maury said. "Hash even boasted about them running the Pecos country."

Jackson grunted. But there was little laughter in his cold gray eyes. He was speculating on the audacity of this killer named Doc Wesley. It had been rumored that the

38

Tenejos were a sanctuary for many of the worst outlaws in the West. Organized into a unit by a man like Wesley they could well become the worst scourage to plague Texas. The Tenejos were a natural hideout, uninhabited, trackless country for the most part with the equally desolate New Mexican Territory and Mexico behind them to provide escape from Texas law.

Jackson's horse suddenly snorted, shaking his head violently, and Jackson came alert instantly. He saw that they had come to the head of the small canyon where Maury's cabin was hidden behind a stand of pines. And he noticed, too, that the day had worn on, made darker by the leaden sky. It would be completely dark in a matter of a few minutes now.

A thin spit of snow came at them as they entered the canyon. Maury edged ahead, driven by that sense of uneasiness. And by a dismal foreboding that sickened him.

The United States Marshal was searching the trail ahead. But the dusk and the sudden snow squall made tracking impossible. He put his roan to a quick pace and was still ten yards behind the smaller man when they broke out of the trees into the clearing.

The candlelight against the window was like a yellow eye seeking them out. Maury breathed a sigh of relief. He looked back and said: "Reckon everything's all right, Colby," and spurred his mount on ahead.

The animal's shod hooves rang on the frozen ground, heralding his approach. Jackson settled back in saddle, but caution made him slip his sixgun into his hand.

Lucy's cry pierced the darkening day, like a knife thrust through the gloom. It was loud, protracted . . . and then it was abruptly cut off by the heavy blasting of a Colt.

Maury's horse skidded and slipped on the frozen earth as the little man hauled back savagely on his reins. The candlelight had been snuffed out with Lucy's cry—the man who flung the door open was only a tall shadow against the interior darkness.

The smoky red flare of his muzzle blast lit up Beaver's face briefly. The bullet hit Maury as he was sliding out of saddle. It spun him around and sent him sprawling.

Jackson, coming up behind, fired at the moving shadow. His slug hammered Beaver back against the door framing. The outlaw brought his Colt up. His bullet whistled past the big man on the roan and Jackson's anwering blast sent him across the threshold in a limp heap.

Maury had regained his feet. He lunged for the cabin and a shot from the inside stopped him. He stood spraddled over Beaver's body, one hand pressed against the door framing.

"*Lucy!*" There was a terrible urgency in his whisper. "Lucy . . . ?"

The gun inside smashed again and Maury fell backward across Beaver's unmoving figure.

Jackson was out of saddle and running at an angle for the door. He was thus out of sight of the killer waiting inside until he lunged across the threshold. And then he was in darkness also and provided no ready target.

Odds Hawley's Colt lashed the gloom in frantic searching. From floor level Jackson fired back, driving his bullets into the shadowy figure above the gun flares.

For a few moments after all sounds of gunfire had faded into the canyon stillness there was a raspy sound of hard breathing. A horrible gurgling. Then this ceased and only the wind made noises outside. The snow came sifting in across the sprawled body of Beaver. . . .

Slowly Jackson got to his feet. There was an ache inside him as he waited, a reluctance to strike a match. He knew what he would find. And the sense of a terrible loss sickened him.

The match flare lasted long enough to show him Lucy Bittering lying in a small, pitiful heap by the table. Her last act had been to sweep the candle from the table, before Hawley or Beaver shot her.

Jackson found the candle and lighted it. Then he walked to the woman and picked her up, her frail body seemingly weightless in his arms. He laid her down gently on the wall bunk and her right hand slid limply over the side. Metal glinted briefly as something she had been holding dropped beside the bunk.

Jackson picked up his badge and held it for a long moment in the palm of his hand. Lucy Bittering, he thought bleakly, was through with worrying about Maury.

The snow was beginning to pile up in tiny ridges against Maury's body when Jackson bent over him. In the darkness beyond Jackson's horse whickered questioningly. The Marshal raised his eyes to look across the darkening clearing to the squall-hidden knoll where the Bittering girl was buried.

He found the double-bitted axe in the shed where he had placed it, and the rusted shovel that had seen little use since Susan's burial. He walked with them to the top of the knoll. The frozen earth yielded reluctantly to the bite of the axe. It took Jackson a long time to dig the graves deep enough for Lucy and Maury Bittering.

He gave Odds Hawley and Beaver a different burial. He found their horses hidden in the thickets behind the cabin and he tied each man across a saddle. Mounting his roan, Jackson led the burdened animals out of the canyon and turned them loose, sending them plunging into the darkness with the aid of several well-placed shots.

The fire in the wood stove had gone out when he returned.

He rustled up more firewood and started a blaze again and stood before the small stove until the warmth drove the chill from him.

He didn't sleep well that night. He lay awake and listened to the snow and knew when it had stopped. The fire went out and cold crept back into that lonely cabin. . . . He could hear his roan and Maury's two animals stamp restlessly inside the meager shelter of the lean-to beyond.

Somewhere out in that cold night a cry rose against the stars . . . the savage lonely cry of a timber wolf in need of a mate. All the small noises of the dark seemed to cease, held breathless by that ancient call.

Jackson smiled and settled back and finally slept.

VII

COLBY JACKSON left the small cabin in the early morning. Behind his roan, on a lead rope, trailed Maury's two cayuses. One was the rangy, line-back dun Maury had ridden, the other a trim, buckskin mare which he used as pack animal.

The snow squall of the night before had sprinkled a thin layer of new snow over the old and in passing had left the morning sky clear. A weak sun poked warming rays over the trail leading out of the clearing.

Jackson closed the cabin door before leaving, knowing he'd not be coming this way again. He mounted and glanced up at the knoll where the fine snow covered the grave he had dug last night and nodded slightly in final tribute to the man and woman who had saved his life.

It was slightly over five miles to Lobo Ravine and the wind had sharpened as he came up to Ten Spot Smith's log outpost. There was a lone animal nosing the rack, a gaunt, ribbed grulla shivering in the pale sunlight. Jackson ran his eyes over the brand by habit and surprise sent a small shock echoing through him.

Bar Y! He studied Harvey Yellen's brand, feeling hope rise up in him and fan out in an aura of anticipation. He dropped his roan's reins over the rack and brushing up against the grulla he noticed that the animal was still warm, which meant that whoever had ridden him had tied up here only a few moments before.

Disappointment dulled the keen edge of his anticipation as he entered. There was a sorry-looking character elbow-leaning on the bar, a gangly youngster as undernourished as the bony grulla tied outside. A long, bony face under a thatch of straw-colored hair, loose, moody lips. A pair of ears jutting prominently under a greasy, torn Stetson cocked far back on his head.

So whom did you expect to see? Jackson thought wryly. *Donna Yellen? Or Marty? Bar Y's cavvy have been scattered over hellangone—this kid probably ran across the grulla somewhere in the foothills. . . .*

The boy was alone at the bar. Smith was not in sight; probably in the back room. There was the odor of frying pork in the air, coming from the kitchen. The kid was looking along the bar, toward the origin of that smell, like some hungry hound dog.

Jackson walked across the dirty floor and the kid turned his head and gave him a quick look. He was nursing a glass of beer and the Marshal saw that he was wearing a black turtleneck sweater under a frayed gray coat and both coat and sweater were out at the elbows. His black trousers were patched in two places and his boots were cracked and the heels runover.

But the Colt .44 in the Missouri holster tilted forward at his narrow waist for a quick left hand draw looked fairly new and scrupulously clean.

The youngster turned fully around as Jackson breasted the bar and this time he gave the Marshal a slow and insolent once-over. His eyes rested for a long moment on the Colt showing under Jackson's unbuttoned coat.

"You look prosperous, pilgrim," he murmured. "Buy me a shot of whiskey?"

Jackson put his hard glance on the boy. Not more than seventeen years old, he figured. Not a grown man yet, either in body or between the ears. But the youngster's pale blue eyes held the scar tissues of a hard life; they revealed a lot of knocking around.

"Sarsaparilla's more your drink, son," Jackson replied. "What are you doing away from home?"

The youngster took this calmly enough. "Minding my own business, grandpa."

Jackson grinned. "Keeps you out of trouble, anyway," he agreed. He turned to face Smith as the outpost owner came into the room, wiping his hands on his apron. Smith's eyes showed a flicker of recognition as he paused across the bar from the Marshal.

"Hombre with the big mouth got home all right?" Jackson questioned. His tone was casual.

Smith shrugged. "They stayed all night, left early this morning. McCoy was nursing a headache with a bottle of whiskey, but he expected to live through it." He reached for a bottle on the shelf behind him. "Whiskey?"

Jackson nodded. He remembered what Maury had told him about McCoy and the fact that he was a Morgan rider threw an obstacle in the way of his decision to ride to the Morgan spread. But the Morgans, Maury had said, knew where Doc Wesley holed up. . . .

"Sorry about the trouble yesterday," he said. "I didn't come in expecting trouble. But Maury was a friend of mine—"

"Was?" Smith's tone held a cautious interest.

"Maury and his wife were killed last night," Jackson said grimly. "Couple of owlhooters name of Beaver and Odds Hawley were waiting for us when we got back. I was pretty lucky. I buried Maury and his wife on the hill, with their daughter."

Smith's face held no expression whatsoever.

Jackson said: "Maury owe you anything?" And added: "He was my friend. I'd like to square up for him, if he did."

Smith shook his head. "A man's debt with me is clean when he dies. If Maury's dead, he owes me nothing."

"Nice sentiment, pop," the kid at the bar put in nasally. There was a note of mockery in his voice, as though this was the key to his character. "In that case, put a bottle of whiskey on my account. I'll pay you—when I can."

Smith ignored him. "You staying on at Maury's cabin, mister?"

"The name's Colby," Jackson supplied. He made a little circle with his glass on the bar top. "Never intended to stay long with Maury. Rest up a while, then I planned to move on. South, I reckon." He looked Smith in the eye. "I'm looking for the Morgan spread. I heard they bought horses and didn't ask questions."

Smith kept a cautious tongue. "Could be." A wisp of smile touched his lips. "If you'd gotten here earlier you could have ridden with McCoy. That is, if he got over the lump you gave him. He and the others were headed for the Morgan ranch." He put the glass he had been wiping down on the shelf and picked up another. "They were a sort of organizing committee, you might say—"

"Organizing?" Jackson's voice held only a casual interest.

"You might ask McCoy." Smith evaded.

Jackson finished his whiskey. There was a subtle change in the light in the room, and glancing toward the windows Jackson saw that it had clouded up outside. A wind was coming up, rattling the loose frames.

"How do I find the Morgan spread?" he asked.

"Take the north trail at the fork at the head of the ravine," Smith directed. "Through Big Bear Pass and down off the south slope of Big Baldy."

He added a few more details. "You'll probably find Big Bear hard going at this time of the year. But the real big snows haven't hit us yet. . . ."

"Reckon I best be moving on then," Jackson murmured. He put money on the bar, glanced at the silent kid. "Give him a square meal, Smith. He needs that more than he needs a drink."

The youngsters raised his head. "I'll be the judge of that," he sneered. He turned to face the lawman. "I was headed for the Morgan place myself. Mind if I ride along with you, big fella?"

Jackson frowned. "If you think that crowbait of yours can keep up, son . . . ?"

"The name's Andy," the boy said angrily. His mouth twisted in a conscious hardness. "Lots of gents know me as the Nebraska Kid."

Jackson's regard was more thorough. He had heard of the Nebraska Kid, but he knew that the killer who went by that name was older than this boy by five or six years. Older and heavier—and meaner. He had studied the dodger on the Nebraska Kid once.

46

GALLOWS GHOST

The boy was obviously using the outlaw's name to give himself an aura of importance. Probably an orphan, cast out on his own, and drawn by the reputations of men outside society—outcasts like himself. There were too many youngsters like this since the War, drifting over the land. . . .

He didn't want this boy on his hands in the grim business which lay ahead of him. But he couldn't just leave this youngster stranded here.

"If you want, Kid," he nodded.

They went outside. The sky was blue-black in the north and although it was midmorning the wind had a sharpness to it that cut into them. Jackson glanced at the ill-clad boy and shook his head.

"I've got a brush jacket in my pack," he said. "And you can throw your saddle on that big dun. That grulla of yours won't last a mile."

The bogus Nebraska Kid stood slightly behind Jackson, his left thumb hooked inside his belt. He nodded and there was a whimsical smile on his homely face.

"Thanks, big fella."

Jackson ducked under the rack. He didn't see what hit him. He didn't even feel the impact of the Kid's Colt. The last thing he remembered was ducking under that weathered pole into an exploding darkness.

VIII

WHISKEY BURNED in Jackson's throat. He coughed and rolled his head away and opened his eyes. Smith's blurred face loomed over him and then the sharp pain in his head made him close his eyes again. He waited until the throbbing eased a bit . . . when he opened his eyes Smith was standing up, glass in hand, frowning.

"You're heavier than I thought," the small man said. "I dragged you inside the door, but that was all I could manage."

"More than I deserve," the Marshal muttered. He had been taken in by a boy still wet behind the ears and his pride hurt as much as his head. He turned and got up, moving slowly, and leaned against the inside wall. He looked at Smith.

"The Kid . . . ?"

"Been gone a half hour. "Took your horses. Left his crowbait."

Jackson nodded. "It figures." He dragged in a long breath. The boy needed to be taught a lesson. Packing a gun and acting tough—

"I wanted to warn you," Smith said. "The Kid ain't nobody to cross."

"Hell!" Jackson sneered. "Seventeen years old, if he's that, Smith! Don't tell me he fooled you into believing he's a tough gun hand?"

"He gutshot the Nebraska Kid," Smith said quietly. "Up in the Panhandle, about six months ago. The Kid didn't take him seriously, either, I heard—"

"This button with the big ears?" Jackson's voice was skeptical.

"That's the story," Smith said. "I hear a lot of them. Most of them ain't exactly true; they're built up a bit here and there. But this one about the Nebraska Kid being outgunned by a youngster with big ears I believe."

Jackson ran his fingers through his crisp black hair, touched the lump on his head. "He's got my cayuse, Smith. And the crowbait he left behind is useless. I'd like to buy one of your horses—"

"Don't have any," Smith cut in. "Figgered it was best not to, long ago. Less trouble, this way."

Jackson turned and flung open the door. The grulla at the rack didn't even lift up its head.

Behind him Smith said: "There's one way you might head him off, Colby. It's a long shot—"

Jackson turned back to the bar. "Let's hear it!"

Smith glanced toward the door. Behind him, from the kitchen, his Indian wife peered into the room, then withdrew.

"Not many know of it," Smith muttered. "There's an old Indian trail runs across Razorback Ridge. You can get up to it behind my place. It's a rough trail and it hasn't been used for years. Don't know how it is at this time of the year. But if you can make it—"

Jackson's eyes narrowed grimly. "Yeah—I can make it!"

"You'll hit Big Bear Pass before the Kid. But I should warn you. There's an old legend about that trail. The Indians call it the 'Way of Death.' They used it only when hardpressed." He glanced at the kitchen, but the woman was gone.

"It's a long chance you'll be taking. If you miss the Kid you'll be stranded in Big Bear Pass, on foot. And at this time of the year . . ." He made a dismal gesture with his hands.

Jackson palmed the side of his jaw in grim reflection. "Give me those directions again," he said bleakly.

Razorback Ridge ran behind Lobo Ravine, a finger of granite reaching out from snowcapped Big Baldy's south flank. The Old Indian trail was grownover and treacherous with winter ice as Jackson came upon it; it crept along the steep west flank of the Ridge and finally heaved over the crest and angled through thin stands of dwarf pine and cedar.

Jackson made the crest, his lungs gulping in the cold thin air. The wind blew with lonely sighing through the trees. It was colder up here on the Ridge.

Far below him lay the small cut of Lobo Ravine, shallowing out to a snow-whitened valley locked between rocky crags. Below him, though he could no longer see it, was Smith's place.

A naked urgency rode the lawman. It was more than the grim need of intercepting the Kid that sent him risking his neck along that ice-slick trail. Goading Jackson was the knowledge that it was almost six weeks since Doc Wesley had shot him . . . six weeks since he had ridden up that still, forgotten canyon of Apache Creek.

Donna Yellen's white face haunted him. Doc Wesley had promised Harvey Yellen he would return his daughter if Jackson rode alone to Apache Creek, but Jackson had no faith in the killer's word.

He thought of Clara Yellen, standing in the doorway of the once proud Bar Y ranchhouse, looking toward the Tenejos looming white and formidable on the horizon. Tortured by thoughts of her daughter and of her son. . . .

Doc Wesley was a madman. Only a madman would have exacted such terrible vengeance, or conceived the fantastic idea of organizing the Tenejos.

Or was he a ghost? The thought broke a bleak smile to the United States Marshal's face.

He'd learn the answer to that grave in Apache Creek when he faced Doc Wesley again. . . .

He turned and plunged ahead, jogging when the trail allowed, climbing when he had to. The wind sighed and wailed along the icy ridge, and over the brooding peak of Baldy the blue clouds massed.

Four miles along the crest of the Ridge trail he reached the end of it!

A bitter disappointment rode him as he paused on the lip of a huge table-flat hunk of granite that ended abruptly at the edge of a gloomy gorge. Ninety feet below him a small, ice-rimmed creek tumbled over black, slick rocks. . . .

Smith had lied! Or else he hadn't known. Jackson's jaw knotted in helpless frustration as he surveyed his plight.

The narrow gorge came down the south flank of the mountain, cutting through the Ridge trail here, parting it like some giant axe had hewn through solid rock. Across the gorge, some eighteen odd feet away and slightly below the level of the spot where he stood, a flying buttress from the opposite wall provided a landing. The trail continued there, curling around the rocky slope.

The Way of Death! This, then, was the reason for its naming. A man got this far and then he either made that jump across the gorge, or died. The Kiowas, Jackson thought, always had a direct way of looking at things.

The wind that came down through the gorge seemed to

mutter old and forgotten tales; in that ineffable sighing Jackson seemed to sense a challenge.

He had gone out for the track team at college and been good enough to make it. But it had been a long time since he had tried a jump like this.

Still, more than one of the hard-pressed warriors who came to this point of no return must have made the jump successfully. Those who didn't made the longer jump to their happy hunting grounds. . . .

He paced out to the edge of the rock and eyed the treacherous footing across the gorge. Below him the icy waters chittered serenely.

Well, he had made his talk and for him, now, there was no turning back. The Kid would be long gone if he retraced his steps and waited at Smith's place for the crow-bait the boy had left behind to recover enough to travel. And quite possibly Big Bear Pass would soon become impassable with heavy winter snows. . . .

According to Smith the trail came out on the south flank of Big Bear Pass. If he made the jump he had his chance to intercept the Kid.

Jackson looked up at the ominous sky. The wind howling through the narrow gorge offered no consolation.

The heavy coat he wore was an encumbrance now. He took it off and dropped it on the ledge, away from him. He felt the icy grip of the wind at once. His hand went down to his gun, jamming it securely into his holster.

Once more he studied the ledge across the gorge, judging the intervening distance like some big prowling cat. Then he turned and paced some fifteen feet back.

He looked up once to the forbidding sky. Then he made his silent run to the overhang and jumped.

GALLOWS GHOST

IX

THE BOGUS Nebraska Kid rode Jackson's big roan stallion up the twisting trail through Big Bear Pass. He was in no hurry, but he rode tense and alert and he cursed the cold and the big stud under him.

Twice the stallion had nearly thrown him. He couldn't relax. The savage animal seemed only to be waiting for one moment of carelessness on his part, one unguarded instant, to whirl and pitch him off.

The sloping walls of the Pass were stubbled with stunted pine, dabbed with snow. They hemmed him in, and he felt lonely and frightened. With no one to watch him the veneer of hardness tore loose and he shivered, his lower lip trembling uncontrollably.

For months he had practiced with the gun in his holster . . . he had lived and eaten with that gun. For sixteen years his mother had been the center of his life—a pallid invalid living in a dour home in St. Joseph. The day she died he wept on her grave and made his silent promise. He left St. Joseph that night. . . .

Now he moved over the face of the land, searching for a man. A man he knew only as a name . . . a man who had deserted his mother, left her to waste her life in bitter withdrawal from it. A woman who had brought him up to hate—to hate the man who had fathered him!

"It isn't healthy," his grandfather had told her. "Poisoning the boy's mind. Let him be, Ellen. You made your mistake when you married him. Don't ruin the boy's life, too."

He remembered those words, but they held no meaning for him—the only thing he remembered was his mother's thin-lipped silence, the deep-scarred hurt in her eyes.

He had run away from his grandparents then . . . he'd been on the move since. His proficiency with the Colt increased, but few men had taken him seriously until the afternoon the Nebraska Kid, face flushed with liquor, had tried to make fun of him as he bellied up to the bar.

He was seventeen that day, that very day, and he looked older than that, if a man didn't look too close.

He had ordered beer and the Nebraska Kid had poured out a tumbler of whiskey and tried to force him to drink it. And he never quite clearly remembered what happened after that, except that he had drawn and shot, at quarters so close his muzzle flare had started a tiny smoldering in the Nebraska Kid's shirt.

The Kid was the only man he had killed. But it gave him a confidence he had not felt before. And shortly after he heard that the man he wanted was in the Tenejos.

A vague feeling of uneasiness made him look back once more. He half expected to see the big man he had left behind at Smith's following, though he knew that this was impossible. There was no animal at the lonely outpost except the grulla he had left tied to the rack, and he knew the animal would have collapsed within a mile if the big man had tried to ride him.

He saw no one else. The trail was plainly marked in the snow, reaching down between the slopes, fading around the shouldering ridge. The Kid sneered. He felt most afraid when he sneered, the way a wolf cub wrinkles his lips in defiance when he is alone and frightened. The sneer on his lips hid the whimper inside him.

Ahead of him, less than a mile now, was the summit of Big Bear. He had listened to Smith's direction, and he know the way to Black Cat Canyon . . . from there on in he'd be on his own.

He didn't care. There was only one thing he wanted from the Morgan brothers.

He shivered again as the wind reached through his threadbare coat. The sun had gone down under a spreading fan of blue-gray clouds which here seemed to rest on the summit. He should have taken the big fella's coat, he thought, and forced his teeth to stop chattering.

He tried whistling through his teeth. Somewhere behind him a wolf howled, and the cry lifted the hackles on his neck and brought a glitter of fear to his eyes.

"Howl, damn you!" he snarled, and patted the Winchester stock rubbing against his right knee.

The roan suddenly stopped, ears pricking forward. A low whinny sounded in his throat. . . .

The Nebraska Kid slid a jumpy glance over the trail ahead. He saw nothing except the tracks of four men who had preceded him; he knew these men were the Morgan riders Smith had mentioned.

He settled back, his knees tightening against the roan's flanks, his muscles tensing for any sudden moves on the big stud's part. "Won't do you any good to call for him!" he snarled. "You won't be seeing that big fella again—"

But a cold foreboding made him twist and look back down that empty pass. He wiped his mouth with the back of his sleeve and turned around.

It took him a long moment to believe what he saw. *It can't be,* he thought, and his mind locked on that impossibility and held him rigid.

Jackson stepped clear of the oak clump flanking the trail. He was less than twenty feet away, and he had been waiting for almost an hour. A big man in gray flannel shirt, and the steady muzzle of a long-barreled Colt eyed the kid.

"What took you so long, Kid?" Jackson jeered.

The Nebraska Kid remained speechless. And the roan, sensing the indecision of the boy, suddenly reared and pitched in a violent explosion of movement.

The Kid's head was nearly jerked from his shoulders. His feet slipped from his stirrups and he bobbed loosely and then fell backward. He landed on the back of his head against the frozen snow and went limp.

Jackson took a step toward him, heard him groan, and relaxed. Momentarily stunned, he thought. He turned as his roan lunged up, muzzling him with warm affection. He patted the sleek neck, sharing the animal's joy.

The dun jerked on his lead rope and the mare, stepping around, nearly trod on the Kid. The boy was stirring. He turned over, then twisted around and came up fast, his hand reaching for his gun. His fingers fumbled at the empty holster; then he spotted his Colt lying a few feet away and he lunged for it.

Jackson's boot came down on his hand as his fingers closed over it; the lawman reached down as the Kid cursed and took the gun away from him.

Jackson said evenly: "You don't give up, do you, Kid?"

The Kid backed away from him. He was like some cornered animal. "You must be the devil himself!" he snarled. "There wasn't a horse at Smith's place you could use. And I kept watching my back trail—"

"You looked back too much," Jackson cut in coldly. He walked over to his roan, opened his warbag, found the brush jacket he was looking for. He straightened, tossed it to the Kid.

"Put that on before you freeze to death," he ordered.

The Kid stepped away from the jacket, his lips twitching defiantly. "Hell with you, big fella! I won't take nothing from you—"

Jackson shoved the Kid's Colt under his waistband, jammed his own gun back into the holster. He took a step toward the Kid then.

"You're pretty big, son," he said grimly, "but not too big for a spanking. Reckon you've needed one for a long time."

The Kid backed further away, his eyes searching the frozen ground. He found a loose rock and scooped it up, raising it threateningly.

"Try it, mister, and—"

He didn't see Jackson draw. There was a flash and a roar and the rock disintegrated in his hand. Pain numbed his fingers. He pulled his hand down to his chest and a cry broke from him, muffled quickly by clamped teeth.

Jackson made a motion with the Colt. "Pick that jacket up and put it on!"

The boy hesitated. He stared into those cold, unwavering gray eyes and a shiver went through him. He licked his lips.

"Put that gun away and then try to make me!" he challenged.

Jackson allowed him this small consolation. He had to leave the boy some shred of pride.

So he holstered his gun, picked up the jacket and tossed it to the Kid.

"All right—put it on, or leave it." He turned to his roan, mounted, then looked back.

The Kid was slipping the jacket on . . . he gave Jackson a sullen, defiant look.

"I should leave you here, son," the Marshal said. "It's

more than you deserve. But you'd never make it back to Smith's—"

"Try me!" the boy snarled. "But if you do, you'd better start sleeping with a hand on that gun, fella. And an eye on your back trail—"

Jackson grinned. "A real bad hombre. Shot the Nebraska Kid and stepped into the killer's boots. You talk tough, son . . . real tough."

The kid eyed him with a sullen look. "How'd you know I wasn't the Nebraska Kid?"

"I knew the Kid," Jackson said. His voice held a growing impatience. "You said you wanted to get to the Morgan place. I'm giving you another chance. Fork the dun and keep a length ahead of me. One length, kid—no more, no less. That plain?"

The Kid shrugged. "Fair enough," he muttered. He walked to the dun, swung aboard.

He waited until Jackson took the dun off the lead rope. "Name's Andy Morse," he offered. His voice was still rebellious. "Andy's good enough. I don't like the son, mister— don't use it!"

Jackson's eyebrows cocked. The boy turned and touched his heels to the dun. Jackson watched the stiff back under the loose brush jacket. He wondered what had brought this boy into the Tenejos.

X

THE PALE SUNLIGHT slanting in through the lone window barely illumined the drafty hallway. It was like a gray and cheerless prison and to the little man in the dark suit the world *was* a prison from which he constantly sought escape.

He paused now with his hand pressing on the wall at the head of the stairs, hearing the early morning clink of glasses as Portigee Joe cleaned up after last night. The stove sent a faint stir of heat up the narrow stairwell, but it did not account for the high flush on Doc Wesley's face.

He coughed suddenly, holding it back with his handkerchief, muffling it behind the wadded ball of cotton. A little man. Some wag once said of Doc Wesley that the two Colts strapped to his hips were one third his weight— that same man had been buried shortly thereafter with another wag's epitaph:

> "Here lies Rod Potter . . .
> he laughed when he
> shouldn't oughta . . ."

Inside the room behind the closed door on his left Wesley could hear the low dismal sound of a woman sobbing. He listened to it with a distant ear . . . it echoed with a vague familiarity. He had heard a woman sob like that often . . .

59

often . . . often . . . the word spun and rebounded in his thoughts.

Too many years ago . . . before he had ridden out to War with the Third Ohio Volunteers. To free the slaves, to wipe out the insolent, bigoted South. He and his brother, Wesley Morse. Only Morse had drifted away from him when he had married. The cleavage of two kindred spirits had been sharp, then. But never entirely clean.

They were twins, his brother and he. Wesley Morse had been born five minutes earlier. The only children of Hannah and Colin Morse.

The sobbing stopped now and in the next room, behind the locked door, he heard someone move and chains clanked. It was as though some wild animal beat against the iron links which held him.

Doc Wesley heard this and knew when the girl started sobbing again. But it made no real impression on his mind. There was a fire in his chest and the urge came again and he smothered the racking cough, forcing it back with handkerchief and grim will. He didn't look at the bloodstains on the white linen cloth he tucked back inside his coat pocket.

From below he heard Portigee Joe's voice call to him with the obsequiousness he had come to expect:

"Doc—yore breakfast, she is ready."

He didn't answer.

His brother Wesley had been more brilliant. Erratic, unstable—but brilliant. A rabid abolitionist. A hater of intolerance. The anomaly here never reached the little man, even as he thought of his brother now. That the man who had hated the South for its racial intolerance had been the most intolerant man of all!

For he had always shared Wesley's views. And when he

received the news of Wesley's death, and of how he died he had at first retreated into a silent, brooding shell.

Wesley hung! Lynched by a band of Texans!

No matter that Wesley had been guilty of deliberate sabotage which had resulted in the murder of sixteen men. For Wesley had been justified. Only the week before Wesley had written him what he had planned and why. The I.O.U. was the biggest silver-producing mine in Apache Creek. And the silver was going into Texas, the slave state of Texas. The long rumblings of civil strife were already in the air. Wesley was in the forefront of the men who advocated war long before the firing on Fort Sumter.

The war came and Wesley was justified . . . the gold camp of Apache Creek faded into history. He had fought with the Ohio Volunteers, and had been captured. The long years at Andersonville were etched enduringly in his memory . . . a political hatred of the South turned into a personal feeling of such intensity that nothing else mattered.

He had wandered over the face of the West after his eventual release, but he never entirely got well. He came to Apache Creek to stand at the silent grave of his brother, and he swore an oath then.

First he would kill the two men directly responsible for the hanging of his brother. Harvey Yellen he found almost within gunshot of the old gold camp. Owner of the Bar Y spread.

But Tom Jackson was dead. Yet Jackson had a son. Doc's sneer twisted his lips. He could not avenge his brother's death on a dead man, but on that man's son he could!

The clanking of chains in the room ceased. He straightened and touched his tie. He was dying. Slowly. An inch at a time, a bit of lung tissue with each wracking cough. Slowly . . .

He had broken Harvey Yellen, left him a helpless cripple, taken away his daughter and his sons. And he had inveigled Tom Jackson's son to the grave of his brother, and killed him as he looked up to see the man who shot him.

Yet it was not enough. He had paid for his brother, but there was yet Texas. A state still racked by the ravages of a lost cause . . . a rebel state which should have been wiped out. Thus thought Doc Wesley, who had taken his brother's name as a pseudonym, a brand-name for his calling.

Doc Wesley. It meant a wanted dodger in a dozen towns. It stood for a little, deadly man with a hacking cough— it meant the fastest, most cold-blooded killer in Texas.

It meant little else. For beyond the hate and the reputation there was little else to the man. The guns and his hate—these had become Doc Wesley. And the cough . . .

From the Tenejos to the Pecos and clear down to the Mexican Border was a raw and widely empty land. A land where Texas law was thinly scattered . . . where a band of hardened outlaws, held together by a master gunhand, could ride roughshod.

This was Doc Wesley's final blow at the land he hated. Texas—big, wide and brawling! Texas—slave state!

Portigee Joe called again, and this time Doc Wesley roused and walked down into the brighter room below. . . .

In the room near the head of the stairs Donna Yellen heard his soft tread as Doc went down. She stood by the window, a blanket wrapped around her, staring with tear-stained eyes at the slope rising toward the gray sky. It was cold inside the room, bitterly cold.

She heard the wild clanking in the next room and her heart twisted and she put her hands to her mouth to choke back the cry rising inside her. How much longer could she stand to listen to that terrible sound?

She crept to the door now and listened. All this was a

nightmare she could not shake off . . . a terrible dream
from which she could not awaken.

She wondered what had happened back home. She knew
nothing . . . not even why she was here.

She put her head against her arms and closed her eyes.
It was summer when the nightmare began . . . it began
with the meeting on the trail to the Jeffrey ranch.

That was the way she met Doc Wesley. A small, bright-
eyed man with a gentle smile, sitting under a tree and
reading. It was a book she remembered: Thomas Paine's
"Age of Reason."

She had pulled aside and inquired if he needed anything and he had come to his feet and bowed. Yes . . .
he was looking for Harvey Yellen. Harvey was an old friend.

She had told him Harvey was her father; he had seemed
pleased and surprised.

"I'll be by as soon as I attend to some business in
town," he had told her. "Please don't tell your father that
you met me. Doc Wesley, Miss Yellen. I want to surprise
him."

So, when the note came, the next day, delivered by a
ragged Mexican boy who lived on Negave Road, she had
obeyed without question. Doc had seemed an old and
mysterious friend.

The note had been penned in a fine script: *"My Dear
Donna: Please excuse the intimacy of my address. But I
seem to have known you a long time. I have had an un-
fortunate accident and if you could come without telling
your father and mother or anyone else, I will be forever in
your debt. It's a small matter, really. And I do so want to
see Harvey. Please come at once."*

There had been nothing wrong, she discovered, when she
arrived at the oak on the road to the Jeffrey place. But the
change in the small man had been a shock.

She had been roughly handled, tied, and brought into the hills and left locked in a room, guarded by a silent, one-eyed man she had come to know as Portigee Joe.

Doc took her out of the room only once; the day he had shot Colby Jackson. By that time her brother, Marty, had joined her as a prisoner in this house.

What satisfaction Doc had taken, in forcing her to witness Colby's killing, a man she had known almost as a brother, she could not fathom. Doc's reasons were his own, bitter, savage and cruel.

He had told her that she and Marty would be set free when he killed Colby Jackson, but he had not kept his word. Nor would he, she thought despairingly.

She listened now against the door and heard the clanking of chains again, and her resolve stiffened in her.

For almost five months Marty Yellen had been kept chained inside that room, like some wild animal. He had fought it at first, and his yells had resounded throughout the house. Marty stood six feet one and weighed one-ninety the day he had been brought here and chained, arms and legs, bolted to the floor of that room. That had been his world for four and a half months—from sour smelling bunk to chain by the window. Portigee Joe brought his food to him and left it within reach and took the tin plate away when he was through.

She had seen her brother three times in that interval, but she was always conscious of him. At first he would yell to her, knowing she was in the next room—talked to her. But finally that ceased, and after a while even the wild bursts of chain rattling stopped.

She lifted her head now, knowing that what she had wanted to do was the only way left. All hope had finally been squeezed out of her and she knew now that she and Marty would not be allowed to leave here alive.

She opened the door and went out into the hallway. She could hear Doc's voice below, extolling bitterly on Lincoln's softness to the South . . . she knew that Portigee Joe, a dull-witted, hairy animal of a man didn't have the faintest idea of what Doc Wesley was talking about.

She edged to the locked door and drew a hairpin and inserted it in the old lock. She worked it around and finally clicked the bolt back.

Marty had shown her that trick himself, once.

She hesitated then. How would she find her brother? She oped the the door and squeezed quickly inside and closed it behind her.

The shrunken figure sprawled on the bunk did not look up. He had wasted a good deal from the vigorous youngster she had known. He seemed shorter and shrunken and older—much older!

She came up to him, her voice aching: "Marty . . . Marty . . ."

He lifted his head. His eyes were dull. They showed recognition, but no spirit.

"Hi, Sis. . . ."

She knelt beside him, her eyes blurred with tears. "Marty . . . I . . . I can't go on any more. Like this. Hearing you . . . seeing . . ."

He lifted his manacled hands. "Like some animal . . ." His voice was a strange, croaking whisper. "Donna—I can't understand. Why . . . why . . . ?"

She shook her head. "He's mad, Marty. Hates Dad for some reason I can't understand. Hated Colby Jackson." She buried her face against his chest. "I was there when he killed him. . . . I called to Colby and he looked up and . . ." Her lips trembled and tears flooded her eyes.

Marty's whisper rasped in that cold room. "Why?"

She shook her head and brushed back a strand of hair.

65

"He'll never let us go free. I believe that now. So . . . I brough you something. . . ." She slipped the kitchen knife from under her blanket. "Do with it as you wish, Marty . . . use it as you see best. . . ."

Hope flickered briefly in his gaze. He took the knife and licked his lips. Then he sat up and slipped the blade under the straw ticking.

"And you?"

"He gives me freedom of the place," she said bitterly. "He knows I won't run away. He's made it plain what he would do to you if I did." She eyed him with a bright gaze. "I can't go on like this any more, Marty. . . . I think I know where Portigee Joe keeps a shotgun. If I can get my hands on it . . . ?"

Marty nodded. Some fragment of spirit crept back into his wasted frame. "Don't worry about me, Sis . . . get away. I told you before—get away. . . ."

She bent and kissed him. Then she turned and left the room quickly. And the boy sat up straighter now, taller . . . he reached under the ticking and brought out the knife and thumbed the blade.

Out in the hallway the girl hesitated. She could still hear Doc talking and she gathered now that he was waiting for someone. He was telling Joe about his plans. . . .

The man was mad! Where it began she did not know. But somewhere in the past Doc Wesley had lost touch with the reasonable world. He heard voices and they were his own voice, the voice of his warped desires, and he rationalized them, making them the basis of his moral judgments.

This man had killed her other brother, Cole. Marty had told her that. What must he have done to her father and mother? What remained of the Bar Y?

66

She saw Colby Jackson's face again, turned up to her, and the memory of it would haunt her forever.

She turned and went back into her room, and waited.

XI

HUBERT MORSE, alias Doc Wesley, fingered the whiskey glass. He was not a drinker; even before the trouble with his lungs he had been sparing of liquor. But he was expecting a visit from the Morgans and he was growing impatient.

He didn't have much time left. He knew from the rising fever in him that a lung hemorrhage could occur at any time. He wanted to get in his last blow at the hated state of Texas before he died.

One raid across the vast Pecos, wiping out all the river towns, looting and burning them.

He was a persuasive talker. In the past three weeks a score of men had come to Portigee Joe's place, singly or in pairs—the lone, hard-bitten breed who hid out in these bleak hills. Men hiding either from the law or from some bitter past . . . men with no future and therefore with nothing to lose.

The cowards didn't come. But the rebels came. And Doc convinced them. Most of them. The very boldness of his scheme caught them. But they hung back, waiting for Doc's assurance. The Morgans.

The Morgans were a power in the Tenejos. They had

been here a long time, and they were a fixture. When a man needed a horse the Morgans provided it. . . .

With the Morgan brothers agreeing to his terms, Doc could swing the rest of the owlhooters in the Tenejos.

He waited now along the bar. Portigee Joe was in the kitchen. He was a strange man, this hulking, dim-witted owner. His real name was Jose Montegra, and he had come into the Tenejos before the Civil War with his two brothers to look for gold. They had worked for the I.O.U. mine when Doc's brother was hung . . . they had had a falling out over a Chinese woman shortly after.

Jose Montegra ran off with the woman; the other two brothers had disappeared.

Jose had come to this lonely spot in the Tenejos and built this place and lived here. His wife died in childbirth —he remained on.

In a corner of the bar he had placed a wooden statue he had fashioned all one summer. A statue of St. Joseph. He set a candle under it and he didn't pass an hour that he didn't kneel before it and pray.

Doc watched him, unmoved. A lout of a man, built like some shaggy bear, kneeling before a wooden figure he had made himself. It was ridiculous, Doc thought.

He started to move toward the kitchen, after Portigee Joe, then paused. The sound of horses coming up to the rack outside turned him toward the door.

He waited. Three men came inside, stamping snow from their boots. And Doc smiled thinly.

Slip Morgan had come, but Doc didn't trust him. He had sent word for Slip to come with his brother, Moose . . . instead Slip had brought two hard-bitten Morgan hands with him.

Slip paused just inside the room and shoved his hat back on his head and waited for his eyes to grow accustomed

68

to the gloom in the room. He was a bony man, over six feet tall, with a scarred right eye, a horsey face. He was thirty-two years old, twenty years younger than the slim, almost debonair Doc waiting by the bar.

Doc said: "You took your time coming, Mr. Morgan. I don't like it."

Slip Morgan's anger showed briefly in his blue eyes. "I came when I could get away," he said curtly. He didn't push the point. Doc Wesley was not the kind of man one crossed. Slip knew that under that seemingly calm exterior lurked a sudden violence—a temper as unpredictable as it was explosive.

"Where's your brother Moose?"

"Moose didn't feel up to the ride," Slip said. He walked up to the bar and pulled off his gloves and dropped them on the counter and blew softly on his bony hands to warm them.

"He's got the miseries. Besides, I do all of Moose's thinking for him."

Doc smiled thinly. He didn't particularly like the Morgans. They were from Pennsylvania originally .... they had drifted into Kansas before the War. He had heard they sold whiskey to the Union army.

"You know why I asked you here, Mr. Morgan?"

The Tenejos outlaw scowled. "Slip's all right with me, Doc. We both know each other well enough to be that familiar."

"You didn't answer me!"

"McCoy told me," Slip growled. "Some damn fool story about organizing the Tenejos. Said you talked to quite a few of the boys—"

"What's so damn fool about it?" Doc snapped.

Slip Morgan reached in his pocket for a cigar. He chewed

on it slowly, holding his anger in check. Behind him his men, clustered about the stove, shifted uneasily.

"I've been in these hills a sight longer than you, Doc," he said. His voice was patient, but it was the restrained patience of an angry man. "My brother and I have a horse spread which—"

"Penny-ante!" Doc broke in. His voice was quick and lights danced in his eyes. His cheeks had an unnaturally red tinge.

"Penny-ante, sure. But we made out. Like a lot of other hombres in these hills." Slip scraped a match and held the flame cupped to his cigar, his eyes measuring the anger in the small man. He had not come prepared to fight, but he was not going to be pushed into something foolish.

"Think about it, Doc. Most of the men in the Tenejos are drifters. They don't stay long. They come into the Tenejos until things quiet down where they came from. Some go back home, others drift on through to the Mexican border. Others just quit running. They build a shack, trap a little, rustle some. They make a sort of living—" He took the cigar out of his mouth and pointed it at the sneering little man. "Now wait a minnit, Doc. I ain't saying it ain't a good idea—up here." He tapped the side of his head. "But when it come right down to getting these men together—"

"They'll come!" Doc said. His voice was thin, deadly. "But some of them are holding back. You know why they are holding back? They want to see where you stand, Mr. Morgan. You and your brother—"

Slip frowned. "Leave things be, Doc," he said patiently.

Doc shoved his empty glass away from him in an angry gesture. "Damn it, Morgan, I didn't come to the Tenejos to hide out like some mole! I've got plans—big plans. We can run this part of Texas—"

"And bring the Rangers in on our neck?!" Slip shook his

head. "When you came you said you had a grudge against the Bar Y. You smashed Harvey Yellen, Doc. And me and my brother took the biggest share of Bar Y beef. I thought that was all you wanted!"

"We got word that a United States Marshal was on his way out here," one of the men by the stove muttered. "Feller called Colby Jackson."

Doc nodded, a thin smile breaking the harsh line of his lips. "You heard right, Lefty. That United States Marshal came—and he's dead!" He waited, letting this sink in. "I killed him!"

Slip Morgan's jaw slacked. The cigar fell from his mouth and trailed ashes down his shirt—he slapped quickly at the sparks.

Doc stepped away from the bar. He was always clean-shaven, always neat—he seemed dapper in contrast with the men facing him.

"I smashed the Bar Y for my own reasons," he said. "I killed Colby Jackson when he came looking for me. It wasn't hard—no harder than the dozen men I've killed."

Slip Morgan wiped his mouth. "Then there'll be others, Doc. The Rangers. They won't let the death of that United States Marshal go unpunished."

"Use your head, Mr. Morgan!" Doc's voice rang with contempt. "A company of Rangers couldn't get within a day's ride of the Tenejos without us knowing about it. In a game like that we have the advantage. We know the hills—they don't. And besides, I doubt if Ranger Headquarters can spare a company of men, not with that trouble they're having on the border."

Slip made a gesture of weary acceptance. "Just one thing, then, Doc. What do we get out of it, Moose and me, if we throw in with you?"

"The Bar Y," Doc said without hesitation. He waited,

smiling faintly, judging the effect of this on the bony man facing him. "You'll get Harvey Yellen's spread, the biggest ranch this side of the Pecos!"

Morgan threw up his. hands. "You lost me now, Doc. I ain't that much of a sucker. Up here in the Tenejos the law has to catch me. But down at the Bar Y I'd be a stitting duck—"

"Listen!" Doc interrupted angrily. "You underestimate me! When you take over the Bar Y it'll be legal. You won't have to worry about the law. Unless you already have a price on your head?"

Slip Morgan shrugged. "Not yet—not in Texas."

"Then you have no worries. Harvey Yellen is a cripple. His spread's shot to hell._ He's got nothing to hold onto anymore. But there's something he wants. I'll wager he wants that more than his spread." He glanced toward the stairs. "That girl and the boy upstairs. To get them back alive, he'll sign anything. He'll sell you the Bar Y for a song!"

Slip Morgan licked his lips in sudden greed. The Bar Y. A chance to get out of the blank wall of the Tenejos. A chance to make a legitimate bid for power. Hell, he knew of other big cattlemen who had started out on as dishonest a basis.

He eyed Doc with a sudden glint of suspicion. "I ain't ever heard you were a hand for charity," he said softly. "What do you want out of this?"

"My own satisfaction!" Doc said. His voice rang with an odd inflection. "I want to get back at Texas!"

Slip frowned. Doc had lost him there. But he now saw the possibilities of Doc's suggestions. Hell, the man was dying, anyway. He didn't take much stock in Doc's ability to organize the Tenejos. But if he could get hold of the Bar Y—?

He thrust out his hand. "Count me and my brother in,"

he said. He turned to the bar. "I'll buy the drinks on it."

Doc nodded. "We'll leave tomorrow. I'll want you along, Slip—at the Bar Y."

Slip said: "Sounds fine, Doc. I'll ride back and tell Moose. We'll meet at the old place, by the Bar Y's northern lineshack."

They had their drink. Then they left.

Portigee Joe went back into the kitchen. Doc walked by the stove and looked out the window. Sunlight made a bright glare on the snow. If the weather held, he could make it to the Bar Y by nightfall. He thought of the surprise his entrance would cause and it gave him a small satisfaction.

Upstairs Marty Yellen waited. He lay on the bunk, staring up at the ceiling. He knew every crack in it. He waited, his muscles tensed and he found himself quivering. A cold sweat came out over him.

It was almost time for Portigee Joe to come upstairs with his meal. He knew this instinctively.

The minutes seemed to drag. He lay still and finally he heard the creaking steps. He slid the knife out from under the mattress and placed it under his left thigh.

There was the rattle of a key in the lock and for a moment Marty thought the hairy man would notice that the door was not locked. But if he did he made no notice of it. He swung the door open and walked inside and gave Marty a bare glance.

He placed the plate and cup of coffee on the chair by the window. The chains on Marty allowed him that much freedom.

A creature of habit, Portigee Joe paused, crossed himself. He was turning away when Marty sat up and doubled over, groaning.

Joe eyed him with the stupid stare of an amiable ox. The boy moaned softly and tried to get up. Joe walked to him. He stood over Marty, frowning helplessly.

The kid straightened and the kitchen knife went into Joe's stomach. It went in deep and then Marty tightened up and his face went green. He gagged and sank back on the cot, his face sweating.

Joe looked at him, his eyes showing a lot of white. His hand went down to the blade—he took a step forward and slapped the boy. The blow knocked Marty against the wall and the boy vomited.

Joe turned away. He walked the length of the room. But his legs weakened as he got to the door. He leaned tiredly against the framing. He was still holding his palm against the knife, as though trying to keep his guts from spilling.

"Doc!" His voice was a loud croak. "Doc . . ."

The man below heard him. Something in Joe's thick voice sent him at a run up the stairs. He came panting into the room, his eyes bright. He took one look at Joe leaning against the framing, saw the knife protruding from between his fingers.

Marty was still retching by the wall.

There was no sympathy in Doc. Only a searching question. Now how did the kid get hold of a knife?

He heard the girl's quick steps on the stairs and he turned in time to see Donna running, disappear around the bend below. He was still trying to catch his breath. The exertion brought on a paroxysm of coughing . . . he fought it savagely, tears in his eyes.

When he recovered he went down the stairs. He walked deliberately and there was a gun in his fist.

He heard her moving about in the kitchen. He came

down the last step in time to see her emerge, an old shotgun in her hands.

She faced him with it, by the end of the bar. Her eyes were bright as his, as glazed with savage determination.

"No more cat and mouse, Mr. Wesley," she said. "No more dying by inches, waiting to learn what you'll do with us. Marty and I—"

He walked toward her, his own gun held down by his side. There was a cold sneer on his face.

"Another step," she cried. Her voice was close to hysteria. "I have never killed a man, but I'll never regret killing you—"

He was close now when she pulled the trigger. She pulled it again and again, the mocking click of the first futile effort ringing in her ears. He reached her and slapped her with the side of his Colt.

Donna fell against the side of the bar and rolled face down in the dirty sawdust and lay still.

Doc stood over her. He stood quiet, breathing with controlled effort. There was a dragging step, a heavy thumping step, on the stairs. He turned and saw that Joe had reached the middle landing—saw him look down at him. Then Joe collapsed and fell in a limp bundle the rest of the way down.

Doc leaned weakly against the bar. Now that it was quiet again he could hear Marty Yellen's thin retching. A cruel smile touched his lips. He could take care of the Yellen kids later . . . tomorrow night, when he faced Harvey Yellen with them!

He turned and went around the bar and poured himself a drink.

XII

SNOW FORCED Colby Jackson and the Kid to hole up on the east side of Big Bear Pass. A mountain squall, it caught them at sundown, roaring in a blinding swirling fury that cut visibility to a few yards ahead of them.

They found a cutback in the slope where a deadfall provided shelter from the storm. Colby brought the two horses under the interlaced boughs and watched the Kid slide wearily from saddle.

The boy shivered.

"Rustle up some wood," Colby ordered. "I'll get some grub from the pack."

They had a fire going in five minutes. There was dry wood under the deadfall, enough of it to keep a fire going all night.

The Kid made a pile by the fire Colby started, then he sat down, Indian fashion, and stared into the blaze. Colby took beans and side pork from the back and set them in the frying pan. There was coffee in the pot. . . .

The Kid didn't look at him. Colby found two blankets and tossed one to the boy. "Better wrap this around you," he advised. "It'll get colder tonight."

They ate in silence. The Kid did not seem inclined to talk, and the Marshal was used to his own silences. He stared into the fire and wondered if Donna Yellen was still alive.

He had gone away to school when she was still a little girl . . . a pigtailed girl who used to run out to meet him when he'd drop by. He hadn't seen the Yellens in the past five years, and it had come as a shock to him that she had grown up. Donna Yellen was now a woman. . . .

Doc Wesley? Whoever he was, he couldn't be the man his father and Harvey had seen hang.

He glanced up in time to see the Kid's eyes close, see him start to slide forward, toward the fire. He reached out and caught him in time and the Kid awakened with a start. For a moment Colby saw the naked fear in his eyes. Then the old glaze of defiance came to the boy's eyes and he tried to pull away from Jackson.

Colby shoved a saddle under his head and eased him down. "Rest easy, Kid," he said gently. "No one's going to hurt you."

The Kid closed his eyes. After a while his breathing grew deep and Colby found another blanket and covered him with it. He heaped more wood on the fire. He knew he would not sleep well, but he was used to it.

The squall passed and the wind died down. There were small sounds in the brush, and the horses stamped restlessly.

Colby settled back against his saddle and fashioned himself a cigaret. He was down to his last drag when the Kid began to breath heavily. He twisted and his voice rose, blurred and mumbling. Suddenly words rang clear: *"Why did you leave us? Why . . . ?"*

He tried to sit up. He stared into the darkness. "I'm going to kill you!" he cried. Then he began to cry. He fell back on the saddle and his sobs were uncontrollable.

Colby left him alone. Finally the crying stopped and the boy slept again. . . .

They saddled and rode with the first finger of light in the Pass. The Kid rode slack in saddle. He looked tired, but there was the hard shell of defiance around his mouth and his eyes had a closed look.

Colby edged close. "How long have you been in the Tenejos?"

The Kid shot him a narrow look. "Long enough."

"Know where the Morgan spread is?"

"Worked there a week, less than a month ago," the Kid muttered. "Earned enough to buy that crowbait you saw at Smith's rack."

Colby frowned. "How'd you get to the Morgans?"

"Walked."

Colby shook his head. "Must be something you want here mighty bad, Kid?"

The Kid smiled stonily. "Is."

Colby changed the subject. "Know where a place called Portigee Joe's is located?"

The boy straightened in saddle. Suspicion brightened his gaze. "No. You headed there?"

Colby shrugged. "Heard a friend of mine was holed up there for the winter," he said carelessly. "But I reckon I won't. I'm headed for the Morgans to pick up some loose change for the two cayuses I picked up. Heard the Morgans were horse traders. . . ."

The Kid's face was hostile. "Better keep a hand on your gun, big fella, when you bargain with Moose Morgan. He's the big dumb cluck, but he'd steal the soup from an orphan's bowl."

"You sound like you know the Morgans?"

The Kid lifted a hand to his cheek. "I know them. I had trouble with Moose—"

"Why are you going back?" Colby's tone was curious.

"I've got no choice," the Kid pointed out. "It's your cayuse. And you're headed there."

Colby considered. Despite the incident at Smith's, he pitied the boy. And he didn't want to involve him in the trouble that might occur at the Morgan place.

"What if I gave you back your gun? Split half the grub with you?" He smiled. "I don't see any need to get you into trouble."

The Kid reined in and looked at Colby. There was a confusion in his eyes, a break in the hard veneer with which he protected himself. He was strangely vulnerable at this moment, as though no one had ever been kind to him before.

"Thanks," he said huskily. "But I'll come with you. I—I got business at the Morgans. . . ."

Moose Morgan blew his nose and eyed the snow-covered slopes rimming the box canyon with morose and cold-dulled eyes. He was a big, hulking man with a face somewhat like the animal he had been nicknamed for, a slovenly man with a paunch hanging over his wide belt.

His head felt like a stuffed feather pillow. He didn't like these hills and he didn't like snow . . . but Slip kept telling him to hang on. Some day they'd have enough to live like kings south of the border.

Moose wiped his dripping nose with the back of his sleeve. Slip had gone to Portigee Joe's to talk things over with that gunslinger, Doc Wesley. Moose spat into the snow in front of the ranchhouse.

Slip was smart. But in some things he was a damn fool. Doc was hell with a gun. But he was dying. His talk of organizing the Tenejos didn't make sense. It would only bring trouble into the hills which so far had been avoided by Texas law.

Hell, if things worked out, he and Slip had their stake. There was still close to a thousand head of Bar Y beef scattered through the lower valleys. Most of them would survive the winter. Some of the boys were down there now, dropping feed. . . .

A lanky individual came from the outhouse behind the stone store-shed. He paused by the ranchhouse steps and glanced at the trail.

Moose said peevishly: "See 'em, Sam? I can't see ten feet with this damn cold—"

Sam grunted. "Yeah. That's Slip—" He stiffened and squinted against the glare of the sun on snow. "Whoa!" he corrected himself. "Two riders, Moose. And I'll be horn-swoggled if one of them ain't that runny-nosed kid you run off about a week ago!"

Moose blinked his rheumy eyes. "Might be trouble, Sam," he mumbled. "Get the boys in the bunkhouse away from their card game. No tellin' who the big gent is."

Sam moved away. The bunkhouse was less than thirty feet from the store-shed. He paused once more to take a long look at the riders. He knew the boy on the dun, but the big man on the roan was also vaguely familiar. He wasn't sure whether he had met this man before, or just heard of him. . . .

Hash McCoy and two others were squatting around the bunk nearest the stove. Hash was saying: "Hit me once more—" when Sam Omish, entering, interrupted. "We got company, fellas. One is the button Moose kicked off the spread last week. The other"—he looked at Hash—"is a friend of yores, McCoy. The big gent who gave yuh the lump on the head."

McCoy swore. He tossed his cards down and stood up, his hand gripping the butt of his holstered Colt.

"You sure, Sam?"

"Take a look," Sam invited, stepping away from the door and waving toward the trail.

McCoy crossed the floor to the door. The other two, after a momentary hesitation, came to their feet and followed.

McCoy sneered. "Didn't expect to see that big jasper again so soon. But this time I'll—"

The man next to him put a quick hand on his shoulder. "Wait, Hash!" He looked closer at the two riders crossing the shallow stream. They were near now, obviously heading for the ranchhouse in front of which Moose Morgan waited.

McCoy shrugged off the man's hand. "I'll take care of the big jasper, Barney. Don't anybody here interfere—"

"You damn fool!" Barney was an older man, at least fifteen years senior to McCoy. His hair was white and the lines in his face were deep.

"You step out there with a gun in your hand and we'll have the bother of burying you!"

McCoy wheeled on him, resentfully. "Keep yore advice to yoreself, Barney! I can take care—"

"No! That's Colby Jackson out there. United States Marshal Jackson!"

McCoy stiffened. The men beside him stared uneasily.

"Barney," McCoy muttered. "Yore seeing things!"

Barney shook his head. "He ain't the kind of a man I'll forget. I was with Henson's bunch on that El Paso bank holdup when Jackson killed Billy Henson. I saw him that day—got a good look at him. That's Colby Jackson out there, on that roan stud."

McCoy licked his lips. He whirled and stomped into the bunkhouse, for the rifle hung over his bunk. . . .

Colby Jackson and the Kid reined in before the Morgan

ranchhouse. Jackson had not missed Sam's quick move back into the bunkhouse. This was a hard crew and there was always the possibility that one of these men would recognize him.

He knew this, but he knew, too, that he would never find Doc Wesley any other way. The Morgans knew where Doc holed out, and so did McCoy. And all he could hope for was a chance to get that information.

Moose was standing spread-legged on the sagging porch in front of the door. His sour smell reached Colby as he and the Kid drew up a few paces away. Whether by chance or design, the Kid reined in between Jackson and the bunkhouse.

Moose looked coldly at the Kid. "Thought I told you to stay clear of this spread," he growled. "What brung you back?"

The Kid shrugged. "Ran into this feller who said he was looking for the Morgan spread. Thought I'd show him the way."

Jackson nodded. Out of the corner of his eyes he caught a glimpse of men crowding the doorway of the bunkhouse and tension gripped him. He'd have to work fast, and he was sorry the Kid had to be in on this. . . .

"That's about the size of it," he muttered. "Name's Jim —Jim Smith. Things got a little too hot up in the Panhandle—"

He pivoted in saddle as Hash McCoy lunged out of the bunkhouse door!

The Morgan rider had a rifle in his hands. He fired a wild shot just as the Kid, whirling his dun to see what was happening, caught the slug intended for Jackson.

The Kid spilled out of saddle, dropping to his hands and knees, his face white, twisted with pain. His horse, and

Jackson's, crowding around him, momentarily hid him from the line of fire from the bunkhouse.

Jackson lunged out of saddle, slapping his roan's side. "Go, boy—run!" His Colt flared angrily at McCoy; he saw the bullet spin the man around, drop him. . . .

Moose swore. He wasn't wearing a belt gun. He turned and started to run back into the house, but Jackson caught up with him. Colby curled an arm around Moose's throat and jerked his bulk around to stand between him and the bunkhouse. His muzzle jabbed hard into the horsethief's side.

"Hold it!" he snarled. "Tell them to hold their fire! I got nothing against you or them!"

Moose yelled: "Hold it, you damn fools! What's all the shooting about?"

Barney's voice came hard and clear: "That's Colby Jackson, Moose! The U.S. Marshal from Houston!"

Moose stiffened. He started to turn but Colby's tightening arm brought a gasp from him.

Colby swore silently. He was trapped. He couldn't make a break with the men in the bunkhouse covering the yard. And besides, he couldn't leave the kid behind—

Moose seemed to sense what he was thinking. He said hoarsely: "You'll never make it out of here alive, Marshal. And when my brother gets back—"

Colby's gun muzzle, jabbing hard into his side, silenced him. The Marshal shot a quick glance down to the Kid who was crawling to the stairs, a hand pressed to his side. He left a trail of blood on the snow behind him.

A shot rang out from the bunkhouse, fired by Barney through the open doorway. The bullet kicked up ice-crusted snow in front of the Kid. He stopped, lifted pain-glazed eyes to Jackson.

"Next shot out of that bunkhouse and I'll blow part

of your backbone out from under you!" Jackson warned grimly.

Moose reacted immediately to the threat. "Hold it, you fools!" His voice was desperate.

There was silence from the bunkhouse.

Colby looked down to the Kid. "Can you make it up here?"

The Kid nodded. He crawled up the steps, still holding a hand pressed to his side. He lurched to his feet, staggered to the door, disappeared inside.

Colby backed into the house, taking Moose with him. Inside, he kicked the door shut, spun the heavy man away from him.

Moose steadied himself against the wall, looked anxiously at Colby. His nose was running. He brought a dirty handkerchief up to it and blew violently. He was feeling too miserable to put up much of a protest.

Colby walked to the Kid who was leaning weakly on the top rung of a kitchen chair.

"Hurt bad?"

The Kid took his hand away from his side . . . his palm was bloody. He shook his head. "Don't think so. Bullet scraped my ribs. . . ." It was an effort for him to talk.

Colby motioned to Moose with his gun. "Take a look at it—put a bandage on it."

Moose hesitated, then started to walk toward the Kid. The boy waved him off. "I'll manage," he said tightly. "Don't want his dirty hands on me, Marshal!"

Colby shrugged. He walked to the window, looked out. The Kid's horse nosed the rail in front, tired, shivering. The pale sunlight glistened coldly on the snow . . . behind the bunkhouse a trail wound over a slope and disappeared.

Moose said: "There's five men inside that bunkhouse,

84

Marshal. And my brother should be back anytime. How long you figger you can hold out?"

Colby looked at him. "Longer than you can!" he said grimly.

Moose caught the implication in Colby's statement; he licked his lips. "Look, Marshal," he said quickly. "Maybe we can make a deal—"

From outside Barney's voice reached them. "Moose! You all right?"

Moose looked at Colby. Colby motioned Moose to the door. "Tell them," he said evenly.

Moose hesitated, then walked to the door, opened it. Colby's gun was at his back and he was in no mood to gamble. "I'm all right!" he called out. "Don't any of you do any wild shooting!"

He stepped back and Colby kicked the door shut. He was intent on Moose and he did not notice that the Kid had moved away from the chair and was now leaning against the wall by the fireplace. Moose's gunbelt was draped over an antler horn, the butt of his Colt jutting from it.

Colby said to Moose: "What kind of a deal?"

Moose glanced out through the window. "There's a saddled horse outside. I can hold off the boys in the bunkhouse for five minnits—"

Colby shook his head. "There's two of us," he reminded.

"It's the best I can do," Moose said harshly. "When my brother shows up it'll be too late!"

"Maybe," Colby said. "But it would be a mistake. I didn't come into the Tenejos for you or your brother. Just one man, Moose—Doc Wesley!" Colby's voice was bleak. "Tell me where to find him and I promise to leave you and your brother alone."

"Moose stared at him. "Doc Wesley—that's who you want?"

Colby nodded.

Moose made a tired gesture of relief. "Doc's up at Portigee Joe's place. My brother's coming back from there now. . . ." He pointed toward the window. "Take that trail north about seven miles, turn left into the small box canyon. Burned out oak at the entrance—can't miss it."

Colby nodded. "All right—it's a deal." He walked to the door, opened it, standing back out of line of fire from the bunkhouse. He motioned with his gun. "Hold your men off—"

Behind them the Kid said: "Just a minute, Marshal!"

Colby turned, eyed the gun in the Kid's hand. His glance took in Moose's gunbelt handing above the Kid . . . the holster was empty.

"You're not leaving without me!" the Kid said bleakly.

Jackson frowned. "Put that gun down!"

The Kid shook his head. His face was very pale, but his gunhand was steady.

"I go first, Marshal—or neither one of us goes!"

Jackson studied the unyielding bitterness in the boy's eyes . . . he shrugged. "All right . . . you go first!"

He turned back to the Moose. "We'll give the Kid five minutes, then—"

Something warned him too late—he started to turn. The side of the Kid's gun smashed against his head . . . his knees buckled and he went down, rolled over and lay still, his hand still clenching his Colt.

Moose turned a startled face to the Kid, shrank from the muzzle aimed at his midsection.

"I've got a better deal for you," the Kid said bleakly. "You get to keep the lawman—I ride out of here alone!"

Moose studied the pale-faced Kid. The boy was hurt

more than he had admitted . . . Moose could tell by the muscle quiver in the Kid's gun arm. He nodded slowly, not understanding why the Kid had turned on the Marshal, and not giving a damn.

"Sure, Kid," he said, "it's a deal."

"I don't want anybody following me!" the Kid warned harshly.

"Nobody will," Moose promised.

He walked to the veranda, faced the bunkhouse. "Barney!" he called. "Come outside! All of you!"

There was a long moment of silence, then Barney appeared, holding a rifle. The others crowded out behind him.

Moose said: "Where's Hash?"

"Inside, on his bunk."

"He got a gun?"

Barney shook his head. He was puzzled. "Hash ain't in no condition to use one."

Moose said: "I got the Marshal inside. I'm lettin' the Kid go. I don't want anyone making a wrong move. You get that?"

Barney nodded.

Moose turned. "It's your move, Kid."

The Kid walked slowly past him, holding his gun. He paused by the side of his horse, looked at the men crowding the front of the bunkhouse. No one moved.

He gripped the pommel with his left hand and pulled himself up, painfully, into saddle. He swayed and for a moment he looked as though he might fall. His lips flattened against his teeth as he fought for control.

He swung the horse away from the hitchrack. He rode slowly for the trail winding up the slope behind the bunkhouse.

Barney moved away from the bunkhouse, started to lift

his rifle. The Kid's back was to him now, providing a tempting target.

Moose said: "Let him go, Barney!"

Barney lowered his rifle. Moose made a motion with his arm. "Come in here—all of you. Give me a hand with the Marshal!"

He stood on the veranda as his men crowded by him, going into the house . . . he watched the Kid ride slowly up the slope and disappear.

If the Kid was headed for Portigee Joe's, he thought bleakly, he'd never make it!

XIII

THE KID RODE north, slumped in saddle. He had no gloves and his hands were cold. He kept his right hand tucked inside his jacket, pressed against his shirt, just above the bullet hole. The bleeding had stopped.

He walked his horse against a wind that cut like a knife. At four in the afternoon dusk was already upon the land. Far ahead one of the taller peaks, towering above the creeping shadows, shone golden in the setting sun.

The Kid shivered. He brought out his right hand and blew on it, but his breath was cold before it reached the skin.

He eyed the trail ahead warily. Moose had said his brother was coming back this way and the Kid did not want to run into Slip Morgan. He knew there'd be small chance of meeting anyone else on this trail at this time of the year. Except for an occasional supply wagon, he had heard, Portigee Joe remained isolated during the winter months.

He topped a small rise and the wind, gusting briefly, scattered light snow down from the towering pines . . . he brushed his eyes for a better look ahead. And now he saw them, perhaps a half mile ahead, just emerging from a clump of trees. Three riders.

They were too far off for him to make out, but he felt they must be Slip and a couple of his riders. The Kid looked around. The nearest shelter was a stand of brush oak about fifty feet off trail. He turned off the trail. He knew he'd be leaving tracks in the crusted snow but he had to gamble Slip would be in a hurry to get back to his ranch and would overlook them.

But he drew his gun and cocked it and rested it on his pommel while he waited behind the screen of brush oak. He shivered again and his dun blew noisily, feeling and disliking the cold.

The Kid patted the animal's neck less with affection than the feeling he was sharing a common plight. "Quiet, fella," he whispered. "I'll see that you sleep in a warm barn tonight."

The animal did not understand, but it seemed soothed by the boy's voice. His head drooped slightly as he waited . . . .

The Kid thought of Jackson now, and felt a twinge of regret. The man had been decent to him . . . he had probably left him behind to die. But he couldn't have the Marshal riding with him. He wanted to see the man they called Doc Wesley alone, before he killed him!

He heard the riders now, moving along the trail . . . there was no conversation between them. They rode at a lope past the point where the Kid had turned off the trail. One of the men turned and eyed the tracks the Kid had made. But it was cold, and he didn't know if they were old or fresh tracks. And he had no reason to fear anyone who had made them. So they rode on, moving quickly out of sight in the gloom. . . .

The Kid waited until he could no longer hear them. The wind sighed in the big pines beyond. Otherwise it was very still . . . and very lonely.

His horse snorted tiredly now and he slipped the gun back into his holster and put his hand under his jacket again. He could feel the cold of his numb fingers through the shirt, against the skin of his side.

The dun plodded out onto the trail and headed into the wind again. He moved at a walk, but he kept a steady pace, as though he knew he was going somewhere where it would be warm. The wind increased as night approached, but the spits of snow that occasionally lashed at the Kid came from ledges and the high branches of trees and not from the clearing sky.

In the patches between the hurrying clouds the stars came out, crystal clear and ice cold. But the Kid viewed them as friends sheltering him from the enfolding darkness . . . he was, after all, only seventeen. And he was a long long way from home. . . .

The trail wound up now across the flank of a granite rise . . . he could sense the depth of the fall off trail but he could not judge it. Whatever lay below was lost in the darkness.

It seemed ages before he came to the lightning-blasted oak and the trail that led past it. He studied the road for a while, for it seemed to peter out immediately against a dark and impenetrable cliff. But the starshine provided enough light for him to see old wagonwheel ruts frozen into rigid mold under the newer snow. And the tracks of three riders, already beginning to be obliterated by the busy wind. . . .

He turned the dun toward the dark cliff and rode until it towered over him. And now he saw that the road led between this granite rise and another just beyond. Now the walls rose high and steep above him, blotting out the sky and the friendly stars. Panic rose in him. *If* Moose had lied . . . ? He could feel the cold getting through to him . . . he was getting sleepy. And already he couldn't feel his feet pressing against the stirrups. From the knees down he had no sensation. . . .

He withdrew his feet and kicked them against the dun's side, but he felt nothing. The dun snorted, but did not quicken his pace.

Somewhere to his left a small stream tinkled through ice-rimmed banks . . . the Kid could hear it but he could not see it. He was too tired to turn back. Somewhere ahead he would find Portigee Joe's—or death.

The canyon walls moved away from him now and a small valley opened up in front of him. The stars appeared in a small patch of sky and this cheered him.

Then he saw the building ahead and slightly below him . . . the yellow lamplight on the old snow outside a window. Smoke curled up from the chimney . . . he could smell it now, rather than see it.

It all looked quiet and peaceful and friendly . . . a warm harbor in a wasteland sea of cold. The dun whickered softly and picked up its pace.

And now the Kid withdrew his right hand and pressed it to his mouth and blew warmth on it, trying to free his numb fingers. . . .

Doc Wesley watched Donna Yellen take his supper plate

away, bring it to the sink. He eyed her morosely, his hand holding a brandy glass. He didn't particularly like brandy, but this was the only drink Portigee Joe had liked and Doc felt he owed this to the fat, unquestioning man who had taken his orders, his tirades and his bad humor without complaining.

Doc was thinking of Slip Morgan's promise and he knew that once word got around that the Morgans had joined him most of the furtive men hiding out in the Tenejos would come to him. Doc chuckled silently at the thought. An army of the damned, to be unleashed at his command against the Texas border towns!

Donna returned, bringing him coffee. She moved lifelessly, her face drained of emotion. He watched her for a long moment, then, as she was about to turn toward the sink he said: "Sit down."

She looked at him, not obeying. Usually he flew into a temper if his commands were not instantly obeyed. But this time he smiled, a small uneven twist of lips in a face that was not used to smiling. He gestured to the chair across from him.

"Sit down," he repeated. "You look tired."

A flicker of contempt passed through her gaze . . . she sank down into the chair, facing him and the door.

He pushed his untouched coffee cup toward her. "Go ahead," he said. "I'll stick to the brandy."

She made no move to touch it. The ugly bruise on her cheek, swollen now, distorted her face.

He said: "I'm taking you home tomorrow."

She stared at him, not believing. He took a sip of brandy. "I promised you I would, didn't I?"

She stared down at the coffee cup. "Yes," she said. She didn't believe a word he said.

A small anger showed in his eyes now. "You should be pleased," he said curtly. "After what you tried to do."

She looked at him now, levelly. "You said you were going to kill me. Me and"—she looked toward the stairs—"my brother."

"I've changed my mind," he said abruptly.

She knew it was not out of the goodness of his heart; there had to be some reason, something he stood to gain from it. But she began to believe him now.

"And my brother?"

He shrugged. "He'll stay here."

"Alone—chained in his room?"

He took another sip of brandy. "He shouldn't have killed Joe."

She closed her eyes and saw the fat man come to the head of the stairs again, look down at her, before he fell . . . she shuddered.

"How long will we be gone?" Her voice was small and desolate.

"Two—maybe three days."

She looked at him, a fear in her eyes. "He'll die. Cold —without food or water . . ."

He finished the brandy and made a bitter face . . . he had never liked any form of liquor.

"I should have killed him—and you, too, long ago," he said coldly. "But I am a man of my word."

Donna began to laugh, hysterically. Neither of them noticed the rider coming up outside . . . her laughter and his gathering rage prevented it.

"You don't know why I hate you, do you?" he snapped. He stood up and looked down at her, unconsciously needing this perspective, for he was a small man.

"My brother was hanged, down there in that ghost town!

By your father! And Tom Jackson! Do you understand, girl? By your father and—"

The rising tide of wrath brought on a fit of coughing. He doubled over the table, bringing his handkerchief out and up to his mouth . . . and for the moment he was helpless.

Donna started to rise. He glared at her, but went on coughing, his wasted frame wracked and tortured. She took a step backward, toward the kitchen sink where a carving knife lay in view on the counter.

She stopped and turned as the front door opened. The Kid came inside. He moved woodenly, on stumps of feet he couldn't feel. His right hand was tucked inside his jacket, under his armpit, in effort to keep his fingers pliable.

He looked at the small man by the table, at Donna halfway to the kitchen sink. He didn't have the strength to push the door shut . . . he just leaned tiredly against it, closing it with his weight.

He said: "Is this Portigee Joe's place?"

Donna was speechless; she nodded.

The Kid moved slowly toward the big pot-bellied stove warming the room. He took his right hand out and brought it up alongside the other and held them both close to the radiating heat.

After a moment he said: "I'm looking for Doc Wesley. I was told I would find him here."

Doc Wesley smothered the last cough in his handkerchief . . . when he lowered it he saw the bright blood against the whiteness and he knew his days were numbered.

But not, he thought bleakly, until he made his raid against Texas!

The girl was looking at him, waiting for him to speak. The Kid said: "Is he here?"

Doc Wesley tucked his handkerchief back into his pocket. Little beads of sweat glistened on his face. He said coldly: "I'm Doc Wesley. Who are you?"

The Kid stared, his freckles dotting the ashen gray of his face making him look older and homelier than he was. This small, rumpled man . . . *this* was the most feared man in the Tenejos?

Doc Wesley had recovered his waspish nature. He snapped: "Speak out, boy! What do you want?"

The Kid was fighting to stay on his feet. He was very tired, and very weak now.

"You," he said. His voice barely rose above a whisper. "I came a long way to find you . . . all the way from Missouri. . . ."

Doc frowned. "Sorry," he said curtly. "But I'm not recruiting boys. . . ."

He sank back in his chair and tipped the brandy bottle over his empty glass.

The Kid took a step toward him, his hands easing down by his side. The gun he had taken from Moose lay in his holster, close to his right hand.

He said: "You don't remember me?" His voice was small and bitter.

Doc eyed him coldly. "Should I?"

"I'm Andy," the Kid said. "Andy Morse."

Doc didn't react at once. It had been a long time since he had heard his own given name spoken . . . he had lived as Doc Wesley too long.

"Andy Morse," the Kid repeated. "Your son!"

Doc's fingers tightened spasmodically around his glass. His eyes burned at the boy as the memories came out of the fog . . . his wife, his family. . . .

He shook his head. "How did you get here?"

"Walked . . . all the way. . ." The Kid's hand came up

95

with a gun in it now and the move, so unexpected, caught Doc by surprise. "All the way," the Kid repeated, "hitched rides, stole . . ."

Doc Wesley was staring at the gun in his son's hand. "You . . . came all this way . . . to kill me?"

The boy nodded. "For what you did . . . to Ma. . . ." He fired then, his bullet smashing the brandy bottle in front of Doc. The small man did not even flinch . . . he just stared at the boy.

Andy moved closer, his gun now leveled at Doc's head. "To kill you," he said, but his voice cracked as he spoke and he tugged at the trigger. The gun went off, but not before he jerked the muzzle away . . . the bullet ripped into the wall behind Wesley.

"All the way," he sobbed, "to kill you. . . ." His knees wobbled and he tried to lift his gun again. "But I can't do it. . . . I can't kill you. . . . I can't kill—my father. . . ."

His legs gave out completely now and he fell almost at Doc's feet. His gun jarred out of his hand and came to rest in front of Donna.

She looked at the gun, at Doc who eyed her now with sardonic appraisal.

"He couldn't kill me," he said thinly, "but you could, couldn't you?"

She didn't say anything, but his answer was in her eyes. He got up and crossed to her and picked up Andy's gun and thrust it inside his waistband.

"Give me a hand with him," he said. "We'll take him to my room." And, as she hesitated, he added bleakly: "This doesn't change anything. I'm still taking you home tomorrow!" He glanced at the limp figure on the floor. "He came out here on his own . . . he can go back on his own! I have no use for him here. Nor do I care!"

96

It did not shock her. Silently, without protest, Donna Yellen helped Doc lift Andy Morse and carry him to Doc's room.

XIV

COLBY JACKSON stared bitterly across the table to Moose who was pouring himself a double shot of raw whiskey into his coffee cup. Colby's hands were lashed to the chair behind him. His head ached dully, but he was still alive. How long he would remain so depended on the tall man standing before the fireplace.

Outside the night wind prowled restlessly like a cold and hungry animal seeking ingress.

Jackson said grimly: "What have you got to lose, Moose?"

The big sloppy man was staring gloomily at his brother He shook his head slowly. "If it was up to me, Marshal, I'd take your word and let you go. But—"

Slip turned and looked coldly at him and Moose lapsed into silence.

Slip came up to face Colby . . . he was holding Colby's badge in his palm. "Your word, Marshal, doesn't mean a thing up here." He eyed Jackson stonily for a moment. "You say you want Doc Wesley? Why?"

Jackson shrugged. "I told you. He nearly killed me at Apache Creek."

Slip frowned. "Just personal reasons, eh? Nothing to do with the law?"

Jackson nodded.

"He told me you were dead," Slip said. He crossed to the window, stared out, thinking, wondering how to turn this to his advantage.

Moose shifted uncomfortably. He felt achy all over and all he wanted was relief from his cold. He gulped down half his spiked coffee.

Slip turned, looked at Jackson. "What about that Kid? Who is he?"

"Claims to be the Nebraska Kid," Jackson said grimly.

Slip walked back to him. "Is he?"

"No. The Nebraska Kid's in a Kansas jail . . . he'll be an old man before he gets out."

"You came here together," Slip said bleakly.

"That's all I know about him," Jackson replied. "I don't know why he slugged me. I don't know why he wanted to go to Portigee Joe's."

Moose eyed his brother. "You didn't see him on the trail, Slip?"

Slip shook his head. "He could have ducked out of sight. We weren't looking for anyone on the way back." He turned as someone knocked on the door. "Yeah," he said harshly. "Come in."

Barney opened the door and came inside. He glanced at Jackson in the chair. "His horse drifted back. We've got him in the barn."

"Is that all you came to tell me?"

Barney's eyes were riveted on Jackson. "No," he said slowly. "Hash McCoy just died."

Slip studied him for a beat, then, callously: "Nothing more we can do then. Bury him."

Barney eyed Jackson. "What about him?"

Slip grinned coldly. "He killed Hash—let him dig the grave!"

Barney nodded. He drew his gun as slip untied Jackson, stepped back.

"When he's through, take him into the bunkhouse."

Barney motioned with his gun. "Let's go, Marshal."

Jackson stood up, rubbed his chafed wrists to get circulation back into his hands.

"Come on," Barney sneered. "You'll get all the workout you need out there!"

Jackson started for the door. Slip said: "Barney!" Barney turned. "I know how you felt about Hash. But I want Jackson alive. Do you understand me? He's riding with us in the morning!"

Barney eyed his cold-faced boss for a long moment. Then he nodded, his voice hard and bitter. "He'll be alive. But that's all I promise."

He turned, shoved Jackson toward the door. They went out into the night.

A man was standing in the bunkhouse doorway. Barney said: "Rollie—get me a pick and shovel. Bring them out to that small rise by the creek."

Rollie headed for the tool shed.

Jackson turned. Barney was standing about ten feet behind him; he pointed with the gun muzzle. "You can walk, or you can run," Barney said. "Either way I'm going to kill you!"

Jackson grinned coldly. "You giving me a choice?"

"Only until morning."

Jackson shrugged. "Fair enough," he said. He started walking, Barney staying ten steps behind him. They walked past the bunkhouse, toward the rise behind the empty corral. The wind blew cold and steady from the dark hills beyond.

"Right here's good enough," Barney said.

Jackson stopped. Somewhere below him water gurgled

softly, but he could see only the tops of cottonwoods, dark and bare against the sky.

Rollie came up with the pick and shovel. He dropped them at Jackson's feet.

"Leave us alone," Barney said.

Rollie glanced at Jackson, then went away.

"All right," Barney said softly. "Start digging, Marshal . . . ."

Inside the ranchhouse Moose was spiking another cup of coffee. Slip eyed him with sour regard. "It'll get to you faster if you drink it straight," he suggested with a trace of anger. "That is, if you're planning to get drunk on me."

Moose shook his head. "This way it's medicine, Slip."

Slip picked up the bottle and eyed it against the light—more than half the contents were gone. "A half bottle of whiskey and a pot of coffee!" He banged the bottle down on the table, his voice angry. "Damn it, Moose, you won't be in any shape to ride tomorrow!"

"I ain't feeling good now," Moose growled. He reached for his handkerchief, blew noisily. "Damn cold," he muttered. "Every year, win, lose or draw. Gets so I can feel it coming on, every year, soon's the leaves start turning. . . ."

Slip shrugged, turned toward the blaze in the stone fireplace. Neither man spoke for a long moment.

"You know know what I'm thinking about?" Moose said finally. Slip didn't turn. He was used to his brother's ramblings.

"I was thinking about them islands that runaway sailor told me about. The one who came through here, about two years ago." He cupped his hands around the coffee cup and stared dreamily toward the window.

"The Sandwich Islands he called them . . . always warm . . . always sunshine. Native girls to be had for the asking

. . . fruit picked right off the trees. No troubles . . . no damn colds . . ."

Slip turned, Moose's ramblings intruding upon his thoughts. "What in the devil are you talking about?"

Moose shrugged. "Nothing, I guess. It's just that I'm tired of living here, holed up like some damn coyotes in these hills."

"Maybe we won't have to stay here long," Slip said.

Moose shook his head. "It don't make sense. Why would Doc Wesley want to give us the Bar Y? What's he getting out of it?"

Slip walked back to the table, looked down at his brother. "I don't care what he *thinks* he's getting. But he's got Harvey Yellen's two kids locked up in Portigee Joe's place. He's willing to trade those kids to Harvey for Harvey's bill of sale—made out to me! That's all I'm interested in, Moose!"

"I don't trust him," Moose said sullenly.

"Neither do I," Slip snapped. "That's why I'm keeping our ace in the hole alive." He turned to look to the window. "I don't know what's between Doc Wesley and that lawman out there. But as long as Jackson is alive, I've got a bargaining hand against Doc!"

In the stillness now, riding the right wind, they both heard the sound of a man digging. Somehow it sent a shiver through Moose.

"I don't know, Slip," he said slowly. "As long as that Marshal is alive, he's dangerous. . . ."

Slip looked back to his brother. "Not with Barney standing over him," he said softly. "I only hope he's still alive— in the morning."

XV

DAWN CAME like a smudge of gray across the bunkhouse windows. Colby opened his eyes. It took a few moments for him to orient himself. He was in a bunk by the window. His shoulder and stomach muscles ached and there were blisters on his hands.

He glanced at the bunk opposite where a guard with a rifle had sat, waiting for him to go to sleep. The man was gone. But there was movement in the bunkhouse and now Barney came over and looked at him.

"There's coffee and biscuits in the galley," he said diffidently. "Or maybe you'd rather travel on an empty stomach?"

Colby got to his feet. "Where is it?"

Barney motioned. "This way." He waited for Jackson to walk past him, to the door, then followed. . . . .

Inside the ranchhouse Moose Morgon was hunched in front of a small mirror, shaving. He looked and felt miserable. He paused, looked at his brother.

"You go, Slip," he groaned. "I ain't up to a long ride."

Slip shook his head. "I told Doc you'd be there." He finished his coffee, stood up. "Now finish shaving and let's get out of here."

He walked to the door and looked outside. The sky was turning pink in the east . . . it looked like it might be a clear day.

Jackson and Barney came out of the galley and walked

toward him. Barney kept his hand on his gun butt. He said: "Rollie's getting the horses, Slip. The big black for you . . . Jericho for Moose?"

Slip nodded.

Barney looked at Jackson. "I'd like to ride the Marshal's big roan? He can ride my cayuse."

Slip shrugged. "It's all right with me."

He turned and looked back into the house. "Moose, you ready?"

"No," was Moose's sour reply. "But I'm coming, anyway."

He came to the doorway to stand beside Slip. Rollie was leading the saddled horses from the barn. Moose glanced up at the sky.

"It's going to be a nice day," his brother said.

"I don't know," Moose said. "I've got a feeling it isn't."

The kid stirred as daybreak filtered into Doc's room. He groaned slightly and Donna, sitting in the chair by his bedside, awoke with a start. She felt stiff and cold and surprised to see that the boy was still alive.

She stood up and leaned over him and put a palm on his forehead. It was still burning with fever. Andy's eyes were open, staring up at the ceiling. But his mind seemed to be wandering between the past and the present.

"I'll find him, Ma . . . I'll find him. . . ." His fingers clutched at the covers. "I promise I will find him for you . . ."

Donna said gently: "It's all right, Andy . . . it's all right. Go to sleep now."

His fingers relaxed slowly, but he kept staring up at the ceiling. His tongue rolled slowly across his parched lips.

He was in church with his mother—but he was only a little boy and he could not understand the stares of the townspeople, nor the tiny whisperings of some of the older, hawk-faced women. But he knew something was wrong as he looked up into his mother's pinched face, the way she sat stiffly on her seat, looking straight ahead . . . he knew something was very wrong and it was because of his father whom he did not remember. . . .

"Stand up straight, Andy," she said stonily, "and don't look around. Don't ever look around. . . ."

Even her voice was strange, harsher than he had remembered. And it seemed to grow harsher, day after day, as she grew visibly older and more bitter.

"It's your father," Grandpa Morse said to him one day. He was older then, old enough to understand now. I know how your mother feels—he deserted her, and you, when you needed him most. But try to understand, Andy. Your father is not to blame. To be pitied, perhaps—but not condemned. Because he is doing what he thinks is right. Let God judge him wrong. . . ."

He was fifteen when his mother died. And he didn't remember a day when he had not seen her crying . . . silent, bitter tears. And on the day they buried her he resolved to find and kill his father. . . .

"I can't, Ma . . . I can't. . . " he cried and he started up in bed, still staring at the ceiling.

Donna's hand was gentle on him, easing him back. Her eyes were abrim with sympathy for this boy. She had stayed by his side during the long night, doing what she could for him.

Doc Wesley had taken the bullet out, but it was too late . . . the wound was already infected, and the infection was spreading.

Behind her the door opened and Doc Wesley came into the room. He was dressed for the weather, a wool scarf around his throat.

104

He came to the foot of the bed and looked at his son and Donna wondered what he was thinking. He looked old and ravaged by his disease, but there was no emotion on his face.

What kind of man can stand by and watch his son die? she thought numbly.

He took out his pocket watch and glanced at it and put it away. "We can't wait any longer," he said coldly. "We'll have to go."

"But he's dying," she said. "We can't leave him alone."

Wesley started pulling on his gloves. His cartridge belt with its twin holsters hung low on his hips, showing beneath his coat.

"There's nothing more I can do for him," he replied. And added unfeelingly: "He should have stayed at home. I didn't ask him to come out here."

She stared at him in dazed horror. "But he's your son!" she said.

"He came to kill me," he pointed out. He looked at the boy, his thoughts masked, his face cold and unfeeling. "If he *is* my son," he added slowly.

The boy twisted slightly and started to whimper. He looked small and helpless now, lying in bed—all the surface toughness was gone.

Doc looked at Donna. "I said we have to go," he said harshly.

"Why?"

"I promised the Morgans."

"They are more important—than him?"

"What I have to do is more important to me," he answered bleakly. "Now put this on!" He flung a heavy mackinaw at her.

She took it and put it on.

Andy Morse looked at her, his eyes filmed with fever

. . . he licked dry, cracked lips. "Ma—I couldn't do it. . . . I couldn't, Ma. . . ."

Donna reached over and put a cool hand on his forehead. "I know," she whispered. She was only a few years older than this boy, but she felt so much older.

"Don't leave me. . . ." His voice was weak.

She glanced at Wesley. He shrugged, motioned to the door.

"I'll be right back," she said, knowing it was a lie and feeling it choke her.

She turned then and walked out, shutting the door on Andy's low, repeated appeal.

The horses were saddled and waiting outside. She closed her eyes for a long moment as Doc Wesley climbed into saddle of his horse. She didn't know if her brother was still alive—she hadn't seen him since the other night. And there had been no sound from his room.

"We're late," Doc said. "We'll have to push the horses to make up time."

She climbed into saddle of the horse beside the small, deadly man. The day was already bright—in a few minutes the sun would be lifting above the high, enfolding peaks.

She looked up to the window of her brother's room and her lips formed a silent goodbye.

In Doc's room Andy stared at the ceiling, his thoughts confused.

"Sorry, Marshal," he whispered. "Have to do it . . . have to see my father alone . . . have to . . ."

The room was cold and soon it would grow colder as the fire in the fireplace died out. . . .

Upstairs chains clanked as Marty Yellen dragged himself to the chair by the window. He looked out and saw Doc and his sister as they rode away. He straightened and tugged at his chains in a wild frenzy until his meager

106

strength gave out, then he collapsed on his bunk and began to sob. . . .

It was a long ride from the Morgan hideout to the Bar Y northern lineshack. Moose and his brother rode up front with Jackson in the middle, trailed by Barney.

The weather had taken one of those late winter changes, shifting overnight from bitter freezing to almost mild warmth. The wind was from the south and the sun, high now, was unobscured by clouds which remained, blue-black and ominous, on the northern horizon.

Everywhere the snow was melting, forming rivulets pouring into the streams. As they came down from the mountains the trail turned muddy and slippery and the horses moved slowly, unsure of their footing.

They paused for a breather on the last foothill ridge overlooking a rolling valley below. The linehouse was about four miles away, hidden from sight by a swell of land. But Colby knew, as he looked at the scene, that the Bar Y range started here . . . a broken, empty empire at the heart of which waited a crippled, bitter man.

He wondered if Donna was still alive. Or her brother. No one could judge the twisted mind of Doc Wesley.

But he knew what Barney was thinking. His was a straightforward, uncomplicated hatred. And Colby knew that Barney had no intention of letting him survive the day.

At Slip's signal they moved on again. The ride had worked off most of Jackson's stiffness and the warmth kept his fingers pliable.

He wondered if the Kid had survived the bitter night and the ride to Portigee Joe's. And if he had—?

The linehouse came into view now, a quarter of a mile away . . . a sagging shack leaning against the slope of a hill. Untenanted, uncared for, the winter winds had toppled the rusting chimney pipe . . . it lay across the pitch of the roof, held there by the thin connection binding it to the pipe coming up from below.

Slip pulled up sharply and the others reined in just behind. He studied the scene, disappointment showing on his face. There was no sign of Doc Wesley, or the girl.

He drew his Colt and fired into the air and the sound bounced back from the nearby hills. But nothing moved around the lineshack and the signal evoked no corresponding reply.

He looked at Moose, slouched over his saddle. "Doc should have been here by now," he said. "He didn't have as far to come."

Moose shrugged. "Maybe he gave up the whole idea." His tone indicated he wished it were so.

"No," Slip said. "But something delayed him."

From behind Moose, Barney said: "That Kid was headed for Portigee Joe's, wasn't he?"

Slip frowned. "That's right. I forgot about the Kid."

"He had a bullet in him when he left," Moose said. "He barely made it into saddle." He shook his head. "Even if he managed to live long enough to get there, what could he do to Doc Wesley?"

"I don't know," Slip muttered. He put his gaze on the hills from which Wesley would be riding. Nothing moved. An uneasiness stirred in him, changing to a slowly growing anger at the thought he might have come here on a wild goose chase. That his dreams of owning the Bar Y had been based on nothing more than the erratic scheming of Doc's twisted mind.

He said: "You and Barney wait at the lineshack, Moose. I'll ride up the trail a piece . . . see if I spot them coming in."

Moose shook his head. "I'd feel worse, just waiting around. Let's all go."

Barney leaned over, patted the roan's right shoulder. "Looks like this cayuse's coming up lame, Slip. He skidded on that ice patch a while back. You and Moose go on ahead . . . I'll wait at the shack with the Marshal."

Slip eyed him and Jackson for a moment, sensing what lay behind Barney's offer. But he nodded, not caring enough to argue.

"Just make sure he's alive when we get back," he said flatly. He turned his mount and headed off, toward the hills. Moose looked at Barney, not believing him . . . but he shrugged and rode off, following his brother.

Barney drew his rifle and laid it across his pommel. He waited a moment, until Moose and Slip were out of earshot, then: "All right, lawman—let's go."

Jackson kneed his horse into motion. He knew that Barney was going to kill him, but he sensed that the man would wait until Moose and Slip were out of sight.

He rode slowly, Barney a few paces behind. The roan Barney rode minced restlessly, showing no signs of lameness. He whickered once to Jackson, questioningly, as though wondering why a stranger was riding him instead of the tall man he had known well for seven years.

The lineshack loomed up, fifty yards away. Its door was open and the tiny prints of rodents were still visible in the snow melting in front of it.

"This is far enough," Barney said. Jackson stopped and looked at him, but Barney had his gaze on the hills. Moose and Slip were out of sight.

He waited a moment longer, studying Jackson . . . he was an older man, hardened and unredeemable. Violence was ingrained in him . . . he knew and lived in these hills the way a lobo wolf did.

"Get down," he said. His voice was quiet, but it had a snarl in it.

Colby didn't move.

"*I said get down!*" Barney cocked the rifle now and rested the barrel on the pommel, the muzzle pointed directly at Colby.

The marshal obeyed. He stood by his horse, waiting. The roan under Barney was eying him, ears pricked forward.

"Now start running!" Barney commanded.

"You heard your boss," Colby stalled. "If you kill me—"

"You tried to get away," Barney interrupted. "What else could I do?"

"You think he'll believe that?"

Barney grinned coldly. "Slip will have to believe it." He raised his rifle. "Now, *run!*"

Colby took a step away from the cabin, then suddenly whirled, his voice sharp and commanding to the roan: "Now, boy—*up!*"

The roan reared up sharply at Colby's command, just as Barney fired. The bullet went wild. Off balance, Barney dropped the rifle and clutched at the saddle horn to keep from being thrown.

He saw Colby dive for the rifle he had dropped and he clawed for his belt gun. But the roan was whirling, trying to shake him off. In desperation he swung his right leg over the pommel and jumped free, rolling away from the plunging hooves of the roan. He scrambled to his knees in time to find himself facing Colby across twelve feet of melting snow.

They fired almost simultaneously. Colby's rifle bullet lifted Barney and flung him backward, his Colt flying out of his hand. He lay on his back, tried to turn over, then went limp.

Colby got to his feet, picked up the gun Barney had dropped. He checked it, replaced the fired cartridge with one from his belt, dropped it into his holster. It didn't feel the way his own weapon did, but it would have to do.

Holding Barney's rifle, he whistled for his roan. The stallion came up, whickered softly. Colby swung up into saddle.

The Morgans had a ten minute start on him. But they were headed for Portigee Joe's, and that's where Jackson had been going, from the beginning.

He clung to one slim hope—that he would find Donna Yellen still alive.

XVI

SLIP MORGAN pulled up and looked at his brother, a questioning frown in his eyes. "Hear it, Moose?"

They were in a pocket of the foothills . . . the lineshack was out of sight beyond them.

Moose sniffed. "Hear what?"

"Sounded like gun shots."

Moose turned in the saddle and looked back the way they had come, then swung back to his brother. "You didn't really expect Barney to keep him alive?"

"Sounded like more than one shot," Slip said uneasily. "I don't like it. Barney doesn't usually miss."

Moose said tiredly. "We can always go back—" He cut himself short as two riders showed up on the trail ahead.

Even at the distance he could make out Doc's small figure, hunched over the saddle of his horse. The girl riding beside him he assumed was Donna Yellen, old Harvey's daughter.

They waited, forgetting about the shots that had echoed faintly behind them. Slip's eyes were hard, searching Wesley's face as they approached.

Doc said testily: "I said to meet at the Bar Y lineshack." He had the arrogant facility of putting people in the wrong, even then they were right.

"We were there," Slip said. "You weren't." He looked at the girl. "What kept you?"

"I was delayed," Doc said. His voice was casual, as though the event was of no moment. He changed the subject almost abruptly. "You came alone?"

Slip hesitated. "No. We brought someone with us. He and Barney are waiting at the lineshack."

"I said no outsiders," Doc snapped.

"I think you'll be glad to see him," Slip replied. "He's been looking for you."

Doc eyed him narrowly . . . something in Slip's voice held a taunt and he didn't like it.

"I make the terms," he said coldly. "If you brought someone else into this, the deal is off."

Moose interjected tiredly: "Aw, the hell with this cat and mouse game, Slip. Tell him it's that Marshal, Colby Jackson."

Doc started. Donna Yellen lifted her head and stared at Moose, a brightness flickering in her eyes.

Doc said harshly: "Jackson's dead. I killed him!"

"Then you'd better take a good look at the man we got waiting for you," Slip said. "If Barney hasn't already killed him!"

Doc stared at Slip. "I saw him fall . . . I saw where my bullet hit. . . ."

Slip shrugged. "Some men are hard to kill." He smiled thinly. "Is the deal on?"

Doc Wesley nodded. "You'll get your ranch," he said. "If there's any fight left in Harvey Yellen, Colby Jackson's body will finish it!"

He reached out and picked up the girl's reins. "Just in case you get some bad ideas," he said coldly. "Remember, I'll kill you before I let you get away!"

They swung away, heading for the slope that walled them off from the Bar Y. . . .

Marshal Jackson topped the ridge as they were riding toward him, a hundred yards downslope. The surprise was mutual, for Jackson had not expected to run into them this close . . . but he was looking for trouble and he reacted quicker.

He fired once, while they were still grouped somewhat loosely together, and cursed downhill shooting which caused him to miss. He wanted Doc Wesley, but he killed Moose's horse instead.

Moose went down heavily, rolled behind his horse. Slip stood up in his stirrups, bringing up his rifle and fired at the lawman on the ridge . . . he fired twice without knowing if he had scored a hit.

Jackson slid out of saddle and the roan lunged away as he flattened behind a rock. Below him Slip was turning his horse. . . .

He had time to sight, and this time he got his man— Slip threw up his hands as Jackson's bullet tore into him and slid slowly out of saddle as his horse plunged away.

Donna Yellen uttered one small cry: "Colby!" She jerked

her reins free of Doc's grasp, dug her heels into the horse's flank. The animal leaped ahead, riding up the slope.

Doc drew and fired in one unthinking vicious move. The bullet knocked Donna out of saddle. She fell and rolled limply a dozen yards from where Moose was crouched behind his horse.

A savage, sickening rage brought Colby to his feet . . . he pumped his remaining rifle shots after Wesley. But the man was crouched low in saddle, and his horse, a fast-moving gelding, was heading back down the trail.

Colby dropped the rifle and drew his gun. Moose took a halfhearted shot at him as he came running down the slope . . . Colby's return fire made him dig his nose into the muddy ground behind his horse.

Colby was thinking of Donna Yellen. He had come this close, only to see her killed. . . .

Ahead of him Moose tossed his gun over the side of his dead animal.

"Jackson! I never wanted this . . . I never wanted any part of this!"

Colby paused, reason taking a bit of the edge from his blind fury. He approached the man slowly, his gun cocked.

"Get up," he said harshly.

Moose heaved up over the carcass, his hands raised shoulder high. He looked over to where his brother's body lay and a sickness came into his already rheumy eyes.

"I told Slip," he said bitterly. "But he wouldn't listen—"

Colby picked up the Colt Moose had thrown away; he motioned the sloppy man away from the carcass, keeping him in front of him as he walked toward Donna. He was within ten feet of her when she moaned. . . .

Hope leaped up in Colby's eyes. He knelt beside her, and now he saw where Doc's bullet had hit, high up on her back. Hunched over the saddle when it hit her, the bullet

114

had glanced off bone, instead of going through. The wound was shallow and painful, but with any kind of treatment Donna would live.

He turned her over and saw the bruise on her cheek and his jaw tightened. Donna's eyes flickered open. "Colby!" she whispered. "Marty . . . I think he's still. alive . . . at Portigee Joe's. . . ."

Colby hesitated. She should be taken to a doctor. If he left her to go to Portigee Joe's. . . .

She saw the indecision in his eyes. "We have to go back," she said. She pushed herself to her feet, clinging to him for support.

"We?" he said grimly. "You can't ride, Donna!"

"I can," she said. "I must!"

He looked at her drawn, pained face. Her fingers dug into his arm. "I lived too long with Marty's face haunting me . . . I don't know now if he's alive or dead. And, God help us, if he isn't when Doc gets back there, he'll kill him!"

Moose shifted uneasily.

Colby swung around to him. "You know the quickest way to Portigee Joe's?"

Moose nodded reluctantly. "I know the way."

"You ride with us," Colby said. "I'll get the horses."

Moose looked at the body of his brother. "What about Slip?" he said.

"We'll bury him when we come back!"

The sun's rays pushed brightly through the half-closed shutters of Portigee Joe's, as though wanting to make up for the night's cold.

Andy Morse stirred, looked up at the ceiling. His eyes were clear. He was no longer shuffling between the past and the present. He knew where he was, and why he was here.

And he knew he was dying.

He stared up at the ceiling, trying to make out the small clanking noise he sometimes heard. It was almost as though there were a chained animal in the room above . . . an animal that moved occasionally, but made no other sound.

Doc Wesley was gone. And the girl who had been with him last night. Who she was he didn't know. But she had been kind to him. He knew this, although his remembrance was blurred . . . her face was mixed up with that of his mother's.

The clanking started up again, the chain dragging softly across the floor above. Slowly Andy pushed back the covers. He had to know. Before he died, he had to know what was up there. . . .

He swung his feet out and onto the cold floor. It took a while before he tried to stand up. The room spun around and a cold sweat came out over his body . . . his knees trembled.

But he waited until the trembling ceased, then he stood up. He was very weak. He took a step toward the door and his knees buckled and he went down to his hands and knees. Then he crawled.

He made the door. He opened it and stepped out into the bigger room and stumbled against the small bar and clung to it, looking slowly around. The room was empty. The house was empty, too, he thought, except for that animal upstairs.

He looked around for a weapon. Maybe, behind the bar . . . ?

He clung to the counter as he inched around it. His head was light now, and he felt no pain. Just a slowly growing tiredness.

He found his gun behind the bar, on a shelf where Doc Wesley had hid it. His gun? It was really Moose Morgan's gun, he remembered. But it was loaded . . . and it could kill.

He crossed to the stairs and crawled up, a step at a time. The clanking had ceased. He paused, panting on the landing. Had he been hearing things? Was he so close to dying that he—

The clanking came again, from behind the door in front of him. Just a small sound, as though the animal had shifted position.

Andy crawled to the door, straightened. He tried the knob, but the door was locked. "Hey!" he said. "What's in there?"

His voice was hoarse and weak. And no one answered.

He lifted the muzzle slowly and aimed at the point where the bolt went into the jamb. He fired. The door jarred open slightly as the bullet tore away the lock.

He pushed the door open the rest of the way and looked inside.

Crouched on the bunk, his hair and beard matted and unkempt, Marty Yellen stared back at him.

The Kid took a step inside, raised his Colt. Marty didn't move. The Kid blinked. "You . . . you're a man . . . ?"

Marty's voice was rusty from disuse. Hopeless. "Who .. are you?"

"Me?" The Kid began to laugh. It hurt him to laugh, but he couldn't help it. After a while he stopped. "I'm Andy Morse," he said. "Doc Wesley's son. . . ."

Outside, now, they could hear the sound of a rider approaching. He was coming fast.

By habit Marty moved, dragging his chains with him, to the window. He looked out, then turned slowly to face the boy in the doorway.

"You're . . . in luck," he said dully. "Your father's coming back. . . ."

A small flicker of anticipation flickered in Andy's eyes. "Alone?"

Marty's voice was choked. "Alone."

Andy turned and closed the door. He made it to the head of the stairs, but he was too weak to go down . . . he eased himself into a sitting position on the top step. From here he had a clear view of the door.

He cocked the gun in his hand and waited. When Doc Wesley opened the door and stepped inside he fired.

Doc Wesley never knew who killed him!

Andy Morse was dead when Jackson arrived with Moose and Donna Yellen. He had slumped sidewise, the gun still in his hand.

Colby took one long look at the Kid, at Doc's small, twisted body, then, at Donna's silent gesture he went up the stairs to Marty's room. He came out almost immediately and said: "He's alive, Donna . . . he'll be all right!"

And Donna Yellen wept softly, sinking weakly into a chair. . . .

It was a day later before Donna and Marty felt well enough to travel. Moose was getting over his cold, and the shock of his brother's death.

He helped Colby Jackson load the bodies of Doc Wesley and his son into a wagon they found in Portigee Joe's shed. With Marty riding behind, and Donna on the seat beside him, Colby brought the bodies to Apache Creek. He found the grave of Hubert Morse's brother, Wesley, and he buried Doc Wesley and his son beside it.

Moose looked at him when they were through. "I'd like to go back for my brother," he said. And Colby nodded.

"I said I wasn't after you," he reminded the sloppy man. "Far as I'm concerned, you're free to go."

Moose shrugged. "I've had enough of the Tenejos, Marshal." He swung his horse around and rode away.

It took Jackson and the Yellen boy and girl the rest of the day to ride down to the Bar Y.

It looked deserted. The corrals were in need of repair . . . the house seemed to sag. Tumbleweeds had gathered against the fence posts and the flower beds were dead.

Marty and Donna looked at the once familiar surroundings and tears gathered in their eyes.

"It looks like . . ." She paused, her voice choked. "They couldn't have gone, Colby . . . they couldn't have given up . . . ?"

He shrugged. "Let's go see."

They rode down the long tree-shaded lane toward the house. A wind began to blow, stirring leaves, moving some of the tumbleweeds.

From the barn a droop-eared spaniel emerged . . . it moved slowly toward them, waiting to find out if they were friend or foe. It stopped. Then, as though life had suddenly been pumped into him, his tail began to wag. He ran toward them, barking joyfully.

"Keno!" Marty said. He dismounted and the dog jumped into his arms and began to lick his face and Marty laughed and cried and pummeled the dog.

Jackson's eyes were on the house. The door opened and a figure showed up in it . . . it was Clara Yellen. She moved slowly to the head of the stairs and looked toward them, shading her eyes against the setting sun.

"Donna?" Her voice was a slender thread on the wind, hoping, yet somehow without hope. "Marty?"

Donna Yellen dismounted. Marty straightened. They stood a moment together, then began running toward that small figure waiting on the veranda.

Jackson remained in saddle. He would go in later, after

Clara and Harvey had a chance to see their children alone. This moment, for them, was private.

He looked around. The Bar Y was shot. But it could be rebuilt. With a lot of hard work . . . and a reason for it.

He smiled. He was through being a lawman. He thought Harvey Yellen could use him. He was quite sure Harvey could.

But he was thinking of Donna Yellen as he rode slowly to the barn and dismounted. A man had to have a reason for what he wanted to do . . . and for him, Donna Yellen was a part of it.